EXAMINE
DO

Her very first day on the ward—and Nurse
Clover Dylan's nursing career seems
ruined. Not only is she accused of helping
her cousin Robin to cheat in his medical
exams but she also manages to insult the
important visitor, Dr Darcy Blamine . . .

EXAMINE MY HEART, DOCTOR

BY

LISA COOPER

MILLS & BOON LIMITED
London · Sydney · Toronto

First published in Great Britain 1984
by Mills & Boon Limited, 15–16 Brook's Mews,
London W1A 1DR

© Lisa Cooper 1984

Australian copyright 1984
Philippine copyright 1984

ISBN 0 263 74757 3

Set in 11 on 12½ pt Linotron Times
03–0784–45,000

*Photoset by Rowland Phototypesetting Ltd
Bury St Edmunds, Suffolk
Made and printed in Great Britain by
Richard Clay (The Chaucer Press) Ltd
Bungay, Suffolk*

CHAPTER ONE

'I KNOW I should have had all my injections before coming to Beattie's, Sister, but my GP wouldn't let me have the ones against typhoid and para-typhoid until I had recovered from the attack of gastro-enteritis I had at camp.'

Sister Scott regarded her newest nurse with a mixture of irritation and amusement. 'So you come on duty for the first time after Preliminary Training School looking half dead and expect to do a full day on a busy ward.'

'I'll work hard, Sister, really I will.' Clover Dylan passed a nervous hand over her apron and looked at Sister with wide green eyes.

'I'm sure you are willing, Nurse Dylan. Sister Tutor gave me an excellent report about you and you achieved high marks in your tests, but that doesn't make you fit to work on a ward as busy and heavy as Ward Ten. Have you any idea how heavy a helpless woman patient can be when she comes back from theatre? How often you will have to walk the full length of the department each day and how many times you will be asked to do things that you haven't learned about? The physical stress is bad enough when you are in first rate condition, but the added calls on your inner reserves make it even more exhausting until you gain experience.'

'I'm feeling a lot better today, Sister,' said Nurse Dylan, trying to ignore the weakness in her legs and the sensation that her head was being sliced off half way down, and had a tendency to float away to the back of the room unless she clutched at it.

'I'll take your temperature, Nurse.' There was to be no argument. Sister had the air of one who knows her own authority and will take no resistance from a new nurse fresh from the relatively carefree existence in the PTS, where all the work was done on floppy models weighing far less than any live patient.

Clover Dylan sighed. The thought of her first day on duty had excited her for months. Winter had gone and she had had a few months to fill before reporting to the Princess Beatrice Hospital in south east London for her nursing training after Whitsun, so she had volunteered to help with a group of deprived children who were going on a camping and caving trip to the Mendips.

It had been a disaster from the first day. The weather was bad, the conditions in the camp far less comfortable than had been expected and the children unruly and with a complete lack of regard for safety. The organisers had been glad to cancel the last few days when rain poured down and made the caves under the limestone hills flooded and dangerous, and most of the children had gastro-enteritis. Clover caught it on her last day, delaying her arrival at PTS, and she had only her vaccination against smallpox and her tests for tuberculosis completed ready for Beattie's, as she had learned to call the famous hospital. In PTS, all the health certificates had been inspected and she had been reprimanded for not having her typhoid immunisation certificate ready.

'I know it isn't really any fault of yours, Nurse,' said Sister Scott, more kindly, shaking down the mercury in the thermometer, 'but when you deal with very sick people, I'm afraid we take it for granted that the staff must be fit and you will get little sympathy if you can't do the job for which you are being trained.' She stuck the bulb of the thermometer under Clover's tongue and looked at her watch. The young nurse sat very still, hardly daring to breathe. 'Relax. How can I count your respirations if you hold your breath. By that count, you are nearly dead,' Sister added, cheerfully. 'That's better,' as Clover let out her breath and gasped, slowly resuming her normal rate of breathing. 'They gave you T and Para. A and B in PTS?'

Clover nodded, unable to speak with the thing in her mouth. It had seemed a good idea at the time. Sister Tutor had sent her to a clinic where a young doctor had not only been very pleased to do the job, but had tried to date her as well. Although she had said no, very sweetly, the encounter had done much to raise her morale and to make her realise that some of the highly impressive men she saw swanning about the hospital in white coats were human and vulnerable to her brand of curvaceous good looks, auburn hair and wide green eyes. But the reality of the after-affects of the injections were best forgotten. She had run a high temperature, her head ached to splitting point and she was as weak as the proverbial kitten. As her time in PTS came to an end, she was staggering about finishing her tests and trying to appear normal, terrified that she would be left behind to join the next batch of embyro nurses, and would lose touch with the friends she had made in her first weeks at Beattie's. It would have meant losing three months seniority as well, and coming from an army family she had vague ideas that loss of seniority held a certain hint of disgrace.

Sister examined the reading and nodded.

'Is it all right, Sister? It could be up after the hot coffee I drank at breakfast,' she added, hopefully.

'It's up a point, but not enough to worry us. I think you'll be fine in a day or so, but I can't have you on my ward looking so fragile. Stay there while I phone Admin.'

'You won't let them take me away, Sister?' It was a cry from the heart.

'No, I shall say that you need a couple of days on light duty but that I want you back here after the weekend. That will cover your day off and two days work either helping Sister Tutor get ready for the next batch of new nurses, or there might be a chance for you on the examination run.'

Examination run? Sister had gone and Clover hadn't the slightest idea what she was talking about. I've done my exams for the present—there shouldn't be any more until Prelim, she thought. She might mean I have to have another physical, but surely they would have done that when I was in bed with the temperature?

Through the frosted glass of the office door, vague shadows flitted about their busy ways, everyone seeming to know exactly what to do and what was needed. Clover envied them with all her heart, knowing that training to be a nurse had been her one ambition since she was quite small. Even her parents, who were wrapped up in her father's army career, had welcomed her decision to go to London to train, and she suspected that they were relieved to have no further responsibility for their blossoming daughter. To them, life in a busy hospital, living in a nurses' home, had an element of nun-like seclusion and safety against the dangers that might beset a young and inexperienced girl far from her family.

'I've arranged it,' said Sister, coming into the office briskly, looking very pleased. 'It will keep you occupied and relieve a more experienced nurse.'

'What do I do, Sister?'

'They want you to report to Outpatients in half an hour. That gives you time to collect a coat and whatever you need for a day away from the hospital. You know, a handbag and some cash in case you are stranded.' Sister smiled at Clover's baffled expression. 'Sorry. I can see that you think I'm mad. Let me explain. You are to go with a minibus full of patients to Bart's hospital where the students are being examined. They have to diagnose patients and we send some of our regulars along for the day. Don't look so alarmed. They are all chronically sick, which means that they can come to no harm on this outing. In fact, they enjoy it and volunteer for it time after time. They are paid a little and given a good lunch and are taken from the hospital here and returned to their homes by whatever means they prefer after the session. You are there to see that they can find the lavatory, have something to eat and come to no harm. You are also a kind of security officer.' Sister laughed. 'You have to be careful that none of the patients tell the students what is wrong with them. They are allowed to answer questions about the conditions they have but they mustn't hint about their symptoms. Some are a bit naughty as they know more about themselves than any fresh student could glean from a cursory examination. The students are permitted to examine externally and to ask questions, building up the case history as they would do in a ward, but of course, we can't let the patients suffer from being handled roughly or having instruments passed into any orifice.'

'It sounds terrifying, Sister. What if one of the patients is taken ill?'

'Most unlikely. We choose fairly uncommon complaints wherever possible. Things that are stable and unlikely to blow up in any way. However, if anyone says they feel unwell, report it to the officer invigilating. He or she will be a doctor and will cope with whatever happens. You *will* be in a teaching hospital, not trying to deliver a baby behind a hedge! You will have a list of patients and their potted case histories, but this must remain for your benefit and no hint must be given to any examinee,' Sister stressed, solemnly, 'The exam results of many young medicos may rest with you, so make sure that they have all the moral support you can give them, but no positive help.'

'Am I allowed to speak to anyone?'

'Not to the students being examined, and you are on your honour not to talk about case histories to anyone at all. It might be wise to go out and have lunch in a café, or in the local pub which, I believe, is very good. It has been known for a desperate student to ply a nurse with roast beef sandwiches and tempt her to give away details, so be on your guard.'

Sister was only half smiling and Clover knew that she had a big responsibility. It would be easier than working on the ward, but she hoped that she could manage to stay the course of a whole day without a real rest.

'If you feel unwell, ask if you can lie down in one of the cubicles, but pick one not being used for the examinations if you don't want students mistaking you for a patient!' Sister dismissed her, telling her to take a coat and not a hospital cloak as she might have to come back by tube or bus if the minibus left early and there were no more patients to deliver back to Beattie's.

Clover emerged from the office in a state of near shock. How would she cope with a group of sick people and having to take them half way across London? There will be a driver who knows about it, I suppose, she thought.

'Dylan!' The hoarse whisper made her start. As yet, she hadn't got used to being called by her surname on duty and she saw the anxious face of one of her own set from PTS watching her. 'Is everything all right?' said Delia Norman, her plump face ready to register shock or pleasure. Clover smiled. Delia was the barometer of any crisis arising from the daily life of the girls in the set.

'Fine,' said Clover, with a bright smile. 'I'm being sent to Bart's.'

'Your poor soul. Is your temperature up again? I thought you looked ill this morning. Can't they do anything here for you?'

'I'm on duty, taking some patients. I'm fine, really, De . . . Nurse Norman. I'll never get used to calling you that on duty. Must rush. Have to be ready in five minutes,' she exaggerated, knowing that Delia would want to gossip. 'How's your ward?' she said, as she walked away.

'Half empty and boring,' said Delia. 'I can't wait for a bit of drama.'

Clover smiled. Delia could make a drama out of any situation and she had no doubt that before they met again, she would have some lurid tale to tell in which Nurse Delia Norman played a leading role.

The nurses' home was silent. The staff on duty were already there and the nurses with days off would soon be stirring for late breakfast, but the corridors were deserted. Some of the floors were given over to medical staff, due to the fire that had destroyed a wing of medical school some time ago, and the authorities, after the first doubts about letting doctors and nurses use the same quarters, seemed in no hurry to rebuild. With more relaxed rules, nurses and medical students mingled freely in off-duty hours, but only senior medical staff lived in the hostel, often using the place as a pied-à-terre if there was a late case of importance or an early operation list.

Students in training were expected to leave the home before midnight. On first hearing this rule, most of the nurses laughed, saying that it was possible to sin before midnight if that was what the powers-that-be suspected might be happening at night, but they came to recognise the value of the arrangements, knowing that after midnight, peace and quiet would prevail, allowing weary nurses to sleep after a harrowing day, to be ready bright-eyed for duty the next day.

Clover took up a light raincoat that wouldn't look out of place in the sun. It was bronze-coloured proofed cotton, cut on manadarin lines and smart enough to wear on any occasion. Also, it wouldn't look wrong with sheer black tights and black shoes if the handbag she carried matched. She checked that she had some money and her cheque book in case there was time for shopping on the way back. I forgot to ask Sister what I do about off duty today, she recalled, but common sense told her that she might have to be on duty until the day's exams were over and so have the evening off.

Her spirits rose as she realised that it needn't be too exhausting. Looking back to the first day when her temperature rose alarmingly and she was hardly coherent, she shuddered. It was probably a good thing to feel ill occasionally. It gave her some idea of other people's suffering.

She arrived at the minibus with her cap neatly pinned to the glowing hair, her dress crisp and new and her watch pinned rather self-consciously to her breast pocket, as if it had been used for checking hundreds of pulse rates and respirations. She felt for her keys and couldn't find them at first. As she checked, her weakness showed again and she fumbled with the catch of her purse, her hands trembling. Suddenly dizzy, she bent her head and closed her eyes for a moment, cross with herself that she had rushed from her room and was now feeling slightly faint. The folder of papers fell from her hand and she stooped to pick them up. One sheet of foolscap eluded her grasp and she reached forward, afraid that some vital piece of a case history should disappear under the minibus. A sharp blow to her shoulder made her fall and a voice that held annoyance mixed with concern swore softly. Hands that were strong and none too gentle picked her up as if she was a rag doll and set her on her feet again. The lost sheet of paper was held in a firm brown hand and a man with very dark hair and deep blue eyes calmly read the contents.

'Do you mind? That is confidential,' said Clover, unsteadily. He regarded her coolly. 'I have to keep that hidden. It's forbidden for anyone to read it,' she babbled.

'So you throw it under the wheels of the bus? Here. I see that you have an acromegaly today.

Better get going. We haven't much time. They'll want to begin.'

'I have to take seven patients.' She stood on the lowest step and counted. 'Five, six, seven . . .' She looked puzzled.

'What is it? We're late enough already without you having to count on your fingers.' The voice was more irritated now.

'I wasn't told that there might be eight.'

'Eight? You said you were expecting seven and there are seven patients in there.' The dark blue eyes were furious.

'But you make eight. I shall have to check the list.'

'Good grief, woman! Do I look like a patient? Driver, let's go!' The man swung his long body into the seat next to the driver after leaning over to push Clover into the body of the vehicle and slide the door shut in front of her red face. The bus started off smoothly, and Clover heard a stifled giggle from one of the women sitting behind her. It was too bad. How was she to know that the man, whoever he was, was not on her list? Nothing had been said about taking another passenger, certainly not a man with so little concern for a nurse on her first day. She glanced at the back of his head. The dark hair curled down over a column of brown neck that disappeared into a fresh blue shirt under a pale tan linen coat.

Who was he? A porter, taken along to help with the patients? A doctor hitching a lift to the exams? The blood rushed hotly to her face again. If he was a student, he had calmly read one of the case histories and had no right to examine the patient concerned. She made a mental note of what he had said. An acromegaly? What on earth was that? A piece of equipment? A condition? It was all too confusing.

She saw a man with a large facial bone structure staring at her from the opposite seat. He gave a slow smile. 'This is my fifth time,' he said, with pride. 'Not many of them get me right.'

Clover pulled her thoughts together and smiled. 'You are Mr . . . ?' She consulted her list.

At once, the others tried to tell her their names and what was wrong with them. Clover stopped them and asked them to speak one at a time. She sensed the tension in the neck muscles of the man in the front seat, as if he was straining his ears to hear what was said. If he's a student, I must be careful, she thought and wondered at the lack of security that allowed such a person to ride with the very patients he might have to examine in the cubicles. But she took consolation in the knowledge that Sister had told her that it was unlikely for Beattie's students to examine people attending Beattie's out-patients. And they were honour-bound to admit if they have seen the patient they were given in some other context, she had said. Even so, Clover spoke in a low voice so that only the patients could hear her.

Mr Brogan was the man with acromegaly, a condition of the pituitary gland that made the facial bones and the hands and feet enlarge in adults.

Clover was only dimly aware of the existence of such a gland but tried to look as if she knew all about it. Mr Brogan was very proud of the fact that he was well-controlled by drugs but the bone structure would never go back to normal. It seemed to give him a feeling that he was superior in some way to his fellows.

'I've got Grave's disease,' said a woman, importantly, and Clover began to see that some of the patients took a pride in being different. Clover looked at the woman's damp trembling hands and protruding eyes. 'They want to take out my thyroid gland as it's working overtime and making my heart flutter, but I'd rather have tablets. I'm Amy Street,' she said.

'And you?' Clover looked at a man with an enlarged head and very crooked spine. He switched slightly when she spoke to him and smiled.

He cupped his ear with one hand, as if deaf. 'I'm not too bad,' he said.

'What's wrong with you?' she said, raising her voice and then glancing with apprehension at the man in the front of the bus.

'Mike Bird. I've got Paget's disease and I'm a little hard of hearing, too. Mustn't grumble, though, they're very good up at the 'ospital.'

Another man had every appearance of being perfectly normal. He was smartly dressed and well built and he said his name was Brian Fields. Clover glanced at the list and saw that he had an inguinal hernia. She smiled and he seemed relieved that he didn't have to tell her what was wrong with him. 'I haven't done this before,' he said. 'They were so kind to my wife last year that when I came in to see if they could do this job for me, I felt I couldn't refuse to give some of my time to Beattie's.' He smiled and spoke of the hospital with such affection that Clover was proud to be associated with the huge and important centre of healing. I'm glad they don't know that as yet I haven't been on a single ward to work, she thought. They treated her as if she was really in charge, although she had a suspicion that the man of whom she was very much aware as the bus crossed London, would take over, given half a chance.

Clover was unfamiliar with the area round the old market at Smithfield and found herself glancing out of the windows from time to time to get her bearings. A woman called Mrs Mona Bright coughed spasmodically and Clover had an uneasy feeling that she had caught a cold. Her breath was forced out as if she needed someone to help her breathe, but she was cheerful and there was no sign of a nasal congestion. Clover learned that she had emphysema and chronic bronchitis, a condition with which she had learned to live, helped by the physiotherapy and drugs supplied by the hospital. It was surprising how cheerful they all seemed, treating the trip as if it was a day out to the seaside or some other favourite treat. The possible exception was Brian Fields, who became more and more withdrawn, as if he regretted being so public spirited.

'It will be a great help,' said Clover, forgetting to

speak softly. 'I'm sure the hospital appreciates people like you giving up their time. We all have to learn and medical students can't learn beyond a certain stage without patients. I have a cousin at Guy's.' She thought for a moment. In the flurry of getting ready for her own training, she had forgotten that she had a relative in the big city. Robin had said something about exams to her at Christmas but she had paid little attention to what he said as they were in a large group of people at a party. She dismissed him from her thoughts and saw once more that the man with dark hair was listening.

'Is your cousin qualified?' asked Brian Fields.

'No. He's got lots of exams to take. I don't expect to see much of him while I'm in London. He's always busy.'

'I don't mind being a guinea pig,' said Brian, 'but I don't think I can stand having lunch in the canteen with the patients. I know I shall have hospital meals when they call me in for my operation, but I think I'd rather find a pub, if that's permitted?'

Clover hesitated. She remembered Sister Scott telling her to eat away from the students. If she met them in the local, they would have no idea that she had brought the bus of patients and so could have no interest in her. 'I'm going to a pub where they sell very good sandwiches,' she said, impulsively. 'I have to stay away from the people sitting the exam, so Sister told me to eat away from the hospital. I only know the name of the pub. Do you know the area?'

He laughed. 'Things are looking up. I shall

introduce you to the best roast beef sandwich in London.'

'I didn't mean that you had to take me there,' said Clover. 'I only wanted you to know that there is such a place.' She wasn't at all sure that it would be ethical to have lunch with one of her charges.

'If you're eating there and I am too, there's no reason on earth why we can't at least share a table, or perch on adjacent stools.' His smile was warm and she smiled at him.

The bus stopped and the Cockney driver said, 'Next stop Bart's.'

Clover helped Mrs Wilder to get down from the step, anxiously watching her faintly blue lips as she caught her breath. 'Don't worry about me, dear. It isn't as bad as all that.' She straightened and walked steadily to the entrance. 'I enjoy coming here. I meet several people I know,' she said, with satisfaction.

The others followed the porter who led them to the hall where the examining cubicles were arranged and Clover hurried after them after picking up her folder and coat. The man with dark hair leaned against the bus, regarding her with sombre eyes. Clover felt her resentment growing. His gaze was far from flattering and as she went by, she tossed her head, very slightly, but he saw the mutinous gesture. His face hardened. 'Nurse,' he called, and she paused to look back. Lazily, he stood tall, seeming to uncoil rather than to stand, with a latent strength that was impressive and rather unnerving. She raised her eyebrows in query, trying to appear calm but finding it suddenly difficult to catch her breath, though from no condition such as Mrs Wilder endured. 'How long have you been at Beattie's?'

'Not long,' she said. She had no intention of telling him that she was only just starting.

'Not long.' His eyes took in every detail of the very new belt, the crispness that comes of new cotton dresses and the unsullied shine of the ridiculous cap that first-year nurses wore at the hospital.

'A few weeks, or a few months?' Clover noticed the slight foreign accent and wondered all the more who he was.

'I don't see that it's any concern of yours,' she said. 'Who are you, anyway?' Her temper was beginning to flare with her resentment. When men looked at her it was with pleasure in their eyes, not this thinly-veiled insolence and dislike.

'A week? A day?' The words came like rifle shots of interrogation and she was forced to reply.

'I began today,' she said, her eyelashes fluttering over her too-bright eyes on to the glowing blush of her cheeks.

'Zut!' he said, with a short laugh. 'And already she dates patients! Heaven help Beattie's if that's the growing trend. Have you no sense of proportion? Or didn't they teach you anything in that cosy little school?'

He stretched and picked up a folder of his own and left her fuming. What right had he, a perfect stranger, a student, or a member of the administrative staff, to be so rude? Was he a student? If so, he must be what was charmingly called a mature student. In the dark hair was the first hint of a grey streak and the lines round his mouth were too experienced for a callow youth. She shivered slightly. That hardness in the edges of his laugh held an echo of someone she had seen after a gruelling army exercise, when a few men were faced with exhaustion and were almost lost. She had long forgotten the incident, or thought she had done so, but she recalled it now, clearly, the hollow eyes, the stretched resistance and the near despair. None of this was in the face of the man with deep blue eyes, but there was a memory of suffering. It might not even be his own suffering, but it was there. Would it disappear if he smiled? she wondered. And shall I ever see him smile?

She hurried after her charges and hoped that he would have finished whatever business he had at this hospital and be gone before she need see him again.

CHAPTER TWO

'How did it go?' Delia draped herself over the end of the bed and bit deeply into a crisp apple. 'It's all right,' she said, smugly. 'I'm only eating fruit. I really am going to lose some weight.'

'You will need all your strength when the ward gets busy,' said Clover. She felt weak and drained after what had been a very strange day for a girl who had had nothing to do with hospitals before entering the Preliminary Training School at the Princess Beatrice Hospital.

'Well, aren't you going to tell me?'

Clover Dylan sighed. Delia was fine in small doses, but she had the habit of hanging on every word and extracting the utmost meaning and possible drama from even the most innocent account of an event. 'It was quite interesting, I suppose, but I had a terrible headache for most of the day and all I want to do is to sleep.'

Delia made herself more comfortable. 'You do look tired. Are you sure that the injections haven't gone wrong? You've been lying on that bed since you came back from Bart's and haven't even undressed properly,' she said, reprovingly, but made no attempt to leave her friend to rest.

'I had a nap as soon as I got back and I feel better. Not hungry, but better. Be an angel and pass me that glass of orange juice. I find I want to drink gallons of that stuff.'

'That looks nice. Can I have some?' said Delia, pouring out a generous amount into a toothglass she fetched from the dressing table. 'It's still fruit, so it can't do any harm.'

Clover sat up and sipped the drink. Her head no longer did acrobatics and her eyes felt as if they might remain fixed into her face for at least another day. She smiled. It would all have been quite amusing if it had happened to a complete stranger. If she imagined herself involved, then it could become masochistic.

'I took the minibus full of patients to the exams and they were a very nice crowd. They even seemed to be enjoying it all,' she said. She sipped again, trying to forget the trauma of meeting the man with deep blue eyes who seemed to haunt her as if he had a grudge against young nurses.

'There was a man on the coach who seemed to have some part in the arrangements. Someone from Admin or he might have been a senior male nurse. Somehow I can't think of him as that, but I couldn't place him. None of my patients knew him but they seemed to think he was on the staff some-where. Some of them have been attending the hospital for several years and know every change of staff and most of the doctors personally. I think he was an official from the examining board, sent to snoop.' She couldn't hide the edge of resentment and Delia picked it up at once.

'Oh, do tell me. Did he tell you off? What did you

do to make him cross?' Her eyes gleamed. This was more like it.

'I didn't *do* anything but drop some papers. He was the one who was rude. He not only made snide remarks about me being new but he read the highly confidential notes I dropped under the bus before we started. I said he shouldn't read them and he merely looked at me as if I was something nasty the cat left on the mat and went on reading.'

'Go on,' said Delia, hugging herself and giggling. 'I wish I'd been there.'

'You're welcome to take my place tomorrow. Yes, they told me to go back tomorrow and take another batch.' Clover sighed. 'I wonder if I made the right decision. I could have joined the army and had a lovely time socially. Dad only encouraged me to come here so that I could join the QA's after I qualify, but I'm beginning to wish I'd opted for a secretarial course which would have gained me entry at a decent level, sooner.'

'What was he really like? Good looking?'

'I suppose so,' said Clover with studied lack of enthusiasm. How could she describe the immediate impact of those dark blue glances? How could she hint at the strength of those hands as they raised her unceremoniously from the ground and put her firmly in her place, in more senses than one?

'He is remote and completely without humour, bad-tempered and mean.' She found it hard not to swallow audibly, as there seemed to be a lump in her throat. 'Quite a lot older than the students, so I don't think he was taking exams.'

'Did you see him again?'

Clover blushed. 'I thought I was doing quite well, when he appeared again and asked if I'd seen about the patients' lunch.' She could almost hear his voice as she told Delia about it . . .

'It's twelve-thirty,' he said.

'I know that. I was told to take them to the canteen at one when the final batch of students have finished,' she said.

He stared at her without smiling and she saw that he was now wearing shirt sleeves and had discarded the smart linen jacket. Dark hairs on the backs of his hands added to the force of his appearance. Like a lumberjack, she tried to tell herself, but she knew that his strength was charismatic and not repellent.

'I was given a list of instructions and I have kept to them,' she said, firmly.

'Did you read all the notes?' The voice was cool and had all the warmth of a coiled snake.

'No, I made a note of names and diagnoses and asked each one if there was anything they might need here.'

His glance became less accusing but she couldn't find any sympathy in the sapphire gaze. 'And what did Mr Cousins tell you about his condition?'

Clover gasped. 'Oh!'

'Oh, indeed,' the voice said, calmly. 'And what condition does Mr Cousins have?'

'He's a diabetic,' said Clover in a low voice.

'Did Sister Tutor tell you anything about diets? About insulin and the link between them?' Would she ever forget the silky menace in those words? 'Did she not impress on you all the importance of a diabetic having meals at specified times?'

'Yes,' she said. 'But its only twelve-forty-five.'

'And he has his lunch at twelve-thirty or he gets hypo.'

Clover looked round the room reserved for patients waiting to take up positions in the cubicles and saw that Mr Cousins was missing. She started for the door leading to the cubicles, although she was sure that the students had finished and the consultants had left for their lunch.

'You won't find him there. I sent him up to the diet kitchen with one of the diet nurses. Fortunately, she had details of his diet and times on her list and she had read *her* instructions. Do you want it said that Bart's breed a more efficient brand of nurse than Beattie's?'

'No,' she said, deflated by his manner and the knowledge that she was partly to blame for the oversight. 'I'm sorry.'

'That at least is an improvement. I was beginning to think that you would be that dangerous type who is always right in her own estimation.'

She looked at him with flashing green eyes, her breast a tumult of mixed emotions. 'I do my best. I can't learn everything at once and, if you'll excuse me, I'll go to lunch so that I can be ready for the afternoon session, or that will be wrong!'

Something like reluctant admiration flickered in the dark depths of those wonderful, terrible eyes.

'Sorry,' he said, calmly. 'You are to have lunch here.'

'Who said so? Who are you to tell me to disobey Sister's orders? I was told to have lunch outside so that no student would talk to me and ask me questions about the patients.'

'I, shall we say, represent the interests of the hospital while I'm here. I say that you have lunch here. I have arranged for something to be sent down so that you are here to receive your flock back again and make sure they are ready in cubicles by two o'clock sharp.' He smiled, bleakly. 'I have sent Mr Field away to a lonely lunch. It isn't allowed, you know, to date patients.'

'I wasn't dating him. I was going to have a roast beef sandwich with him and pay for my own, if that's of interest. Anyone would think this was Victorian England. I had no idea that Beattie's would be so stupidly archaic.'

'What a stormy petrel Beattie's has caught this time,' he said smoothly, with a hint of amusement.

'Better a stormy petrel than a . . . a . . . stuffed shirt of a civil servant,' she said and turned her back on him.

She heard a sound at the door and a nurse came in bearing a tray. She smiled and put it down on the table by the window and hurried out again, without a word. A hand on Clover's trembling shoulder made her flinch. 'I'm sorry,' she murmured. 'I suppose you are doing your job.' She turned, her eyes full of tears. 'But I wish you'd give me credit for trying. At least I want to do well—

but how can I if I lack experience?'

His hands fell lightly on to her shoulders. 'You could be right,' he said. 'I was forgetting that you have been ill.' His mouth descended on hers for a butterfly touch and was as swiftly gone as a Chalk Blue. He led her to a seat. To her embarrassment, there were two salads on the tray, two plates of thin brown bread and butter and some fresh fruit. From a bag, he produced a can of Guinness and began to pour it into two glasses. 'You see, we are both tied to our jobs.'

'I hate stout,' she said, ungraciously.

'You'll drink it,' he said. 'You need some real colour in those cheeks, not the flush of anger or sickness.'

And she drank it all and, this time, didn't resent his words. 'How did you know I was ill?'

'I hear most things,' he said, attacking his salad with an enviable appetite. Clover picked at her food and ate the fruit, unable to talk or to think clearly . . .

'And after lunch, we had another full session in the cubicles,' she told Delia, omitting every other detail of lunch with the man to whom she could put no name and who aroused such restless feelings in her heart. He annoys me and that's why he stirs me in such a strange way, she decided. 'It was a very busy day, Delia. I want to get some sleep now, so if you'll kindly get your great bottom off my feet, I'll go and have a shower.'

'Nurse Dylan?' called a voice from the stairs.

'Yes,' Clover shouted down to the hall where a nurse had answered the telephone. 'Oh, damn! Who can that be?'

'It might be your ogre,' giggled Delia, following her as if she might otherwise miss something of interest.

'Goodnight, Delia,' said Clover, firmly. 'Don't you think you should check up on Vilma? She might have had a *very* exciting day.'

'I'd forgotten her. You could be right, Goodnight, sorry I can't stay.' Delia walked away, rubbing a second apple on her dress to polish it.

'Clover Dylan here,' said the weary girl who could think of no person she knew who was near enough to the hospital to want to telephone her.

'Hi there! Remember me?'

'Alex! Where are *you*? I thought you would be deep in lectures or exams.'

He laughed. 'I find Birmingham slightly boring. I'm coming down for the concert at Wembley and I thought I'd check to see if you are still alive.'

'It's good to hear your voice,' she said, with some truth. Normally, she wasn't all that pleased to see him, but after the kind of day she had endured, even Alex, the boy her brother had known at school and who had dated her a few times, was better company than craggy men with sombre eyes and no feelings.

'How are you? Do they treat you well there?'

Clover could hardly believe that this was Alex, the person most likely to be voted selfish chauvinist of the year by all his friends. He was actually anxious to know if some other person than Alex Smithers was all right!

'Nice room? Lots of lovely nosh? Short hours and lots of free time?'

'I didn't know you cared,' she joked.

'Seriously, Clover. Have you a nice big room?'

'What if I have?' she said, with a growing suspicion that Alex had not changed all that much after all.

'Nothing. I just thought you could let me put my bed roll down on your floor.' He chuckled. 'Unless, of course, you've got over your silly prejudice about sharing your bed with a friend.'

'I still like my bed to myself, thank you,' she said, coldly, 'And I can't offer you my floor either.'

'Go on, force yourself. Anyone can do that. Promise to be good, if that's what you want. No hanky-panky in the small hours unless you say so.'

'Alex, I am new here. I have already had a very hard day and am in no mood for you. I can't ask you to stay as there are rules about students being out of rooms after midnight. It isn't the same as a hall of residence in university. Honestly, we have to work hard and the rule is sensible. I might ask if there is a guest room somewhere, but I'm a bit junior to expect favours.'

'What's the difference? Most nurses I know have their own flats away from the hospital and some have live-in boy friends.'

'Not here. There are some non-resident staff but they are more senior and trained. While we are training, unless we are married and can live near, which is discouraged, we live here.'

'Sounds like a lot of stuffed shirts running the place. How old-fashioned can you get?'

Clover found her lips twitching. Stuffed shirts seemed to be in fashion. She thought of the man with curling dark hair and firm cool hands. 'Stuffed shirts often know what they are talking about, even if we resent them,' she said.

'I shall arrive and you will have to make room for me,' he said. 'I'm hitching down tomorrow and the concert is the day after that, so I'll be staying two nights.'

'Alex!' she almost shouted down the line, but he had hung up. She fumed silently as she went back to her room. It was no use telling him that she couldn't help. Alex had always expected his own way and he was no more mature than a seven year old. Ah well, she thought, I can think of that tomorrow.

Her head buzzed with sleeplessness and utter exhaustion as she slipped into bed later, having read the notes of all the patients she had to take with her in the morning. Two were women who would need to be examined physically and she now knew that a nurse had to be in attendance when a female patient was examined by a male student. Not really necessary, perhaps, but a reassuring touch and one of which she approved. I must put them in cubicles next to each other so that I can keep an eye on both of them, she decided, sleepily. She smiled. No diabetics tomorrow and there would be patients from another hospital with another nurse in some cubicles, as this would be the really busy day.

. I'm beginning to think it out for myself, she mused. I wonder if he will notice my new efficiency? If he is there, if I see him again, if he even notices me . . .

The bliss of having a clear head and feet that had no leaden soles made Clover dress with care and she even found herself humming softly as she fastened the silver buckle on her trim navy blue belt, drawing it in to her neat waist and putting the finishing touch to her smart appearance. Her hair went into its smooth daytime style with no effort and her skin looked clear and healthy for the first time since her injections. I think I'll live, she decided and banged on the door of her neighbour, Vilma Mantice.

'You look better.' Vilma regarded her with satisfaction, her dark eyes soft and friendly. 'I prayed for you last night and the Good Lord heard me.'

'It all helps,' said Clover lightly. At first, it had seemed strange to have a girl with such decided religious views in the set with the other girls, but she had proved to be a good nurse in the school, a very entertaining companion and a thoroughly nice person. The fact that from her West Indian face there issued a voice with heavy undertones of Liverpool now seemed irrelevant. Vilma was always ready with sympathy and advice, for she was slightly older than the rest of the set and training for State Registration in order to marry her missionary boy friend and return to a country that was hers by tradition, but which she had never seen.

'I'm feeling lot better,' said Clover. 'I wanted to talk to you, Vilma. Last night, an old friend of my brother's rang and said he was coming here for a concert. He took it for granted that I could find him a bed and I don't know what to do. Do you know of any guest rooms here? I can't think that the Sister in charge of the home would welcome students sharing rooms with nurses.' She saw that Vilma was shocked. 'Not that I have any intention of him sharing my room, but what do I do if he arrives, complete with bed roll and a hopeful expression?'

Vilma frowned as they walked down to the dining room. 'Ask at the lodge. Claude might know. He seems to know everything about this place.' She glanced at her watch. 'We ought to eat first and you could call in on your way to the minibus. You'll have more time than me to do that.'

They collected trays from the counter of the cafeteria and found places in the line of nurses waiting. 'Just in time,' said Vilma, as the line grew visibly and extended beyond the pile of trays at the end of the food counter. 'I hope you eat a little more than you did yesterday. You need building up, my girl.'

'I feel a little more hungry. Oh, good. I like their scrambled egg.' Clover took a hot plate and the food, together with fresh toast and cutlery and they sat at a side table where another of the set, Rosalyn March, was keeping places for them.

'You are up early. Couldn't wait to get on with the bedpans?' she said.

Rosalyn smiled. 'I was pleasantly surprised by day one. What about you two?'

'I was on Children. Very good for me as I ought to learn all I can about children and their complaints,' said Vilma. 'Hugo says that most of my work might well be with children.'

'But that isn't for ages, yet. He must know that you will have to go through all the departments that we have to work in before you take your finals,' Rosalyn persisted.

'I know. I'm afraid that I might spend some of my time dreaming, if I work in places that won't be useful in our work when we are married.'

'Can you wait that long? Can't you get married now and still train?' Secretly, Clover wondered whether this wasn't all a bit personal.

'I don't think so. Hugo will have to go away for a year in the middle of my training and I would rather wait until we can have a home together.'

Rosalyn regarded her with some amusement. 'If I caught my man, I'd want to be with him all the time. I can't think it right to be so patient. If I was in love, I'd need everything, including the physical part.' Vilma blushed.

'Don't tease her,' said Clover. 'It's refreshing to find someone who isn't intent on popping into bed at the first opportunity.'

'Someone bugging you?' said Rosalyn.

'A friend of my brother's wants to come and stay. He is an absolute curse. He tried to get me into bed and finds me very amusing when I say I don't sleep around.' Vilma pursed her lips. 'He rang last night and announced that he will be here today when he's hitched down from Birmingham.'

'Is he a student?'

'Engineering. He knew Ralph at school and came home sometimes. We went to the same parties and he was interested in the Army when he finishes at university, so that made him all right with Dad,' she added, with a faint smile. 'Dad can see no wrong in him, but I find him a nuisance.'

'What are you going to do with him?' Rosalyn laughed, showing perfect teeth in a wide red mouth. Her slightly caustic wit had enlivened many evenings in PTS and she had the added advantage of some experience with the Red Cross as a cadet before coming to Beattie's. 'Why not put him in Delia's room? That would keep her quiet for a while. Oh, God, not at breakfast.' They watched Delia weaving her way towards them with a laden tray.

'Hello,' she said, brightly. 'I brought some extra toast in case someone was hungry.' She sat down heavily. 'What were you all laughing at?'

'Nothing,' said Rosalyn. 'I thought you were on a diet.'

'I am. I only brought extra for you and Clover. She ought to eat up. Thin as a rake. It can't be good for her.' Delia tucked into to her eggs and toast, looking hopefully from face to face.

'Sorry to disappoint you. Nothing happened in the night. Nobody was robbed, raped or sleep-walked. We all woke up unsullied in our little beds and have now exactly ten minutes to be on duty.'

'You *are* silly,' said Delia with a mouth full of toast and marmalade. 'Anyone would think I'm nosy.'

'You, nosy?' Rosalyn looked at her in mock surprise. 'I'll tell you one thing.' Rosalyn lowered her voice and looked round as if to make sure that there was no other person listening. 'We are going to have a *man* living on our floor.'

'We're not!'

'It's a fact. A student is coming tonight, with no place to lay his head, and he wants a charitable nurse who loves students to let him sleep in her room. I wondered if you might volunteer.'

'You're joking.' Delia looked uneasy. 'You are joking?'

'Don't torment the girl,' said Vilma. 'A friend of Clover's is coming and we are going to find him somewhere to sleep, that's all. If you want to catch Claude before you have to leave, you should go now, Clover.'

'Is that the time?' Clover caught up her notes and handbag and the cotton raincoat she had taken on her other trip and fled towards the lodge. The small window overlooking the driveway was open and she tapped on the sill.

The shrewd face of the porter who had been at the Princess Beatrice for more years than seemed possible appeared at the hatch, lighting up with interest as he saw that this was one of the new batch of nurses about whom he knew very little at this

stage of their careers. He offered his help eagerly,
curious to find out what made the pretty green-eyed
nurse look worried.

'Can you tell me if there are any guest rooms for
visitors here?' she asked.

Claude scratched his head. 'They have them on
Childrens' and some of the acute wards,' he said.

'Not relatives of patients,' she said. Suddenly,
she didn't want this man to know about her affairs.
'If my cousin came to London to stay, I would want
somewhere for him to stay. He's a medical student.
Is there a room in the medical school that he could
use?' she added with a flash of inspiration. That was
it. If they thought that Alex was a relative and a
medical student, that could be easier. She dismissed the small deception as unimportant. After
all, she was trying to find some means of having
Alex to stay that would put no strain on her morals
or her hospital discipline. She convinced herself
that if Robin, her real cousin, wanted to come and
stay, the problem would be as she had described it.
To the hospital authorities, one student was much
like another even if one was medical and the other
an engineer.

'Well, I don't know. If he knows one of the young
men in the medical school he could doss down
there, I suppose.'

'He's from another hospital,' she· said. 'He
doesn't know any students here and I haven't had
time to meet any, yet.' She blushed slightly. It
sounded as if she might be hunting for boyfriends.
Claude grinned. 'I thought you might know of a

solution,' she said, with dignity, 'But if you can't help, I have to go.'

'Give me his name, Nurse, in case he rings or wants to get in touch. I'll see what I can do.'

To give his name was the last thing she wanted to do. It would give the situation a certain inevitability and substance that she didn't want. 'He'll be ringing me at the home. Don't bother, Claude. Thanks for your help but I'll think of something.' She escaped before the porter could reply, flashing a dazzling smile at his disappointed face as she went. If he knew the name it would be common knowledge—just one more item of news for Claude to exchange with his cronies he met in the local after duty.

The minibus was ready with four patients inside. A car drew up with two more and the driver of the minibus was standing by the cab smoking a cigarette while they waited for the last one on the list. The acromegaly was back with the emphysema lady but the others were fresh. Clover noticed that the name of Mrs Street, the Grave's disease patient, was crossed off her typed list and she wondered if she had refused to come or if she was ill. Once more, Clover felt the responsibility of her position, wondering what she would do if one of her patients was suddenly ill while they drove to Bart's.

I would have no idea what was needed, she thought. If anything happened, they would expect me to help just because I wear uniform. Even the way they talk to me shows the respect they have for Beattie's and they look on me as an efficient representative of the hospital. If only they knew that I know less than they do about the diseases on this list. Graves disease. She tried to recall what she had read about it in her bemused state last night before sinking into sleep. Thyro-toxicosis caused by an over-active thyroid gland situated at the base of the throat and governed by the pituitary gland in the skull. Treatment, surgery. She frowned. Mrs Street had refused surgery because, as she confided to Clover, she had drugs to control it, except for her heart beating too fast, and she couldn't be away from her family for weeks at a time as she had an invalid husband to look after.

Perhaps the husband was ill, she thought, and tried to think of other matters. It was strange how important it was to know if Mrs Street was all right. She looked around her and asked the lady with emphysema if she knew why Mrs Street was not coming.

'Didn't you know? She was admitted last night to Ward Ten for stabilisation. Her pulse was so bad when the students took it that none of the examiners would believe it possible,' she added, with something like proud envy. 'Then one of the high-ups took it and they made her go into Beattie's.'

'Oh, poor Mrs Street.' Clover looked up at the huge building. Somewhere in there, a woman was worrying about her invalid husband. Someone will do something, she thought. The social services took care of such matters, didn't they?

'That the lot?' asked the driver as the last patient was settled in a seat.

'I suppose so. That's everyone on my list,' said Clover Dylan. She hesitated in the open doorway and glanced back at the hospital. 'No passenger today?' she ventured, half dreading his reply.

'Passenger?'

Clover noticed for the first time that this was not the driver who had taken them yesterday. 'The driver had someone with him yesterday,' she said.

'I haven't been told to wait,' The driver swung into his seat and started the engine. Clover pulled the sliding door over and locked it. She took her place in her seat and began to read the notes again, making sure she could put a name to each of her patients. She barely heard their conversation as the bus found its way through the crowded streets of London. She didn't see the red buses and the cheeky taxis finding gaps in traffic that were almost impossible to negotiate. Her thoughts were full of the day ahead and under it all was the disturbing news that Alex of all people might be coming to make use of her.

She recalled him as he had been when she last saw him. His hands were on her arm in a familiar, caressing manner and his voice held a bantering tone that was both a challenge and an invitation. In vain, she had tried to convince him that his attentions were unwelcome but he took no notice. I think I slapped him, she recalled with amused surprise, and smiled.

'Thinking about your boyfriend, Nurse?' said one of the women with an arch smile.

'Anything but,' said Clover with feeling. And

yet, if Alex did come, wasn't that what everyone would think? He knew so much about her because of her brother that he could convince anyone that he knew her very well indeed, perhaps too well for just friendship. She was sickened at the idea but knew that there was little she could do about it. She could find no way of stopping his visit. Perhaps he would find all the passing cars unwilling to give lifts.

Her depression deepened. Birmingham was on a major motorway and in this good weather there were many travelling reps who welcomed the company of another man in the car. Knowing Alex and his ingenuous smile, which charmed people until they knew him, he would get to London in record time. She could imagine what Alex would say. 'I'm hurrying to get to London to see my girl friend. Yes, training at Beattie's and hasn't been very well.' Anyone would try to help him.

The bus arrived at the now familiar entrance and Clover felt much more confident than she had done the last time she showed her charges into the room where they could relax. One by one, she took them to change and to lie or sit on the examination couches with magazines until they had to endure the ministrations of hot-handed and very nervous young men and women, all striving to gain the coveted qualifications necessary for them to pursue the career of their choice.

'Hello,' said a nurse she had seen on the last visit. It was heart-warming to be greeted as if she really did belong as a part of this new life. Her pulse quickened. The former thrill of anticipation grew again with her new strength and the awareness of her position. It would be a good life after all. She would work hard and try to satisfy the most stringent needs of the hospital. She would be a success and make a good career. She sighed. If only Alex were in Australia or some other distant place where he could do her no harm.

She sat with one of the new women who seemed a little nervous now that she was actually on the couch. Clover patted her hand, comfortingly.

'It's good to have you here, Nurse. You're ever so calm. I expect this is all routine to you.'

Nurse Clover Dylan smiled. Alex could go to hell. It was people like this who would prove her worth, sooner or later. If he came to Beattie's she would cope, as she must learn to cope with her whole future.

'Everything will be all right,' she told her patient. 'Just remember that the doctors examining you will be very nervous and will need your help.'

'I didn't think of it like that. I think I might enjoy it.'

The first rustle of papers and the grinding of chairs on the tiled floor announced the arrival of the consultants ready to confront each student with their obvious Olympian power. 'And what have we here?' boomed Sir Horace Ritchie, the newly re-tired consultant gynaecologist from Beattie's, as a scared man from another London hospital placed a trembling hand on the woman's abdomen to feel the enlarged uterus just palpable under a roll of fat.

Clover smiled encouragingly but said nothing. It

was almost a personal triumph when the student diagnosed possible fibroids which would have to be taken away surgically.

'What else could it be?' The man flushed and looked helpless. 'Well, you've seen enlarged abdomens before, haven't you?'

The poor boy glanced at the grey hair of the woman on the bed. 'She could be pregnant, I suppose,' he said.

'Pregnant? Madam, do you think you are pregnant?' The elderly surgeon had a twinkle in his eyes. The patient shook her head, her eyes wide with sudden fear. 'It's all right, I don't think so, either, and nor would this doctor if he was in his right mind and not petrified of me.' He turned to the student. 'Before you make a diagnosis like that, you ask if the lady is married.' He beamed. 'Are you married, Madam?'

'No, sir,' she whispered.

'You see, my boy, even in this time of profligacy and licence, there are women who are not married and who have only to be seen for it to be realised that they lead blameless lives.' He shook her hand, with old world courtesy. 'My thanks, Madam, for your invaluable help. You have nothing there to worry you.'

He swept out with the student close behind him to discuss the case further away from the patient. 'In any case, you would never accuse your grandmother of being pregnant, my dear boy,' he added.

As Clover listened, she became more and more fascinated. It was clear which students would, as doctors, inspire confidence and do well. Others had a lot to learn about bedside manners and the gentle touch and she wondered from which medical schools they came. Someone mentioned Guy's and she looked up, startled, but not expecting to see the face that stared at her from the waiting room. 'Robin,' she said. 'What are you doing here?'

A man in a beautifully-cut dark suit stood by the door and he turned sharply to see who she was addressing. Her cousin came forward. 'Clover, I have to talk to you. Am I glad to see you.'

'I can't talk to you now. Meet me in the pub in half an hour,' she said. 'I want a few words with you, too.' A sudden solution to her problem presented itself. If Robin could take Alex to the medical school at Guy's, it would solve her difficulty. She smiled, brightly, and he relaxed, turned away and left her to finish her work, but the man in the dark suit barred her way.

'Oh, it's you,' she said, hardly recognising the sleekly dressed man who confronted her. Her heart sank. It was obvious that once more, she was not his favourite person.

'What do you think is going on here? This is a serious place of learning where budding doctors hope to pass enough exams by honest means to be a credit to the profession.'

'And I'm doing my best to help,' she said.

'By hob-nobbing with students and passing on information about the cases?'

'No, of course not.' Her cheeks flamed. 'That

was my cousin. I haven't seen him for months. I had no idea he would be here today.'

'I was chatting to him. He seemed worried and I tried to put him at ease. Many of them get cold feet before they go in there,' he added. 'He told me he was at Guy's and I find that today, it is Guy's students examining Beattie's patients. Now isn't that a coincidence,' he said, with the silky menace she had come to dread.

'I had no idea he would be here. I didn't know he was taking exams,' she said, almost in tears.

'You may go to lunch with him, but under no circumstances can you come back here after lunch. I shall make it my business to tell the invigilators that he must examine cases only from St Thomas's when his turn comes. That will make sure he meets no Beattie's cases and so it will remain fair. But I shall also let his medical school know about this and, of course, your own matron must hear of it, I'm afraid.

Through her tears, she saw the set mouth and the dark blue eyes that now were devoid of anger but filled with a great sadness that nearly broke her heart. 'Who are you?' she whispered.

'Does it matter?' he said, wearily and walked away.

CHAPTER THREE

'NURSE!' Clover Dylan turned sharply and saw that the sister in charge of the examination room was consulting a list. 'Going to lunch? That's right.' She paused and the new nurse felt as if she stood at the edge of a precipice waiting to be pushed over, but Sister smiled. 'If you'd just tidy the main desks where the consultants make their notes before you go, I'd be grateful, Nurse. I see that some of Beattie's patients have to get away and we have an influx of new cases so it isn't important for them to stay after lunch.' She handed four case histories to Nurse Dylan and made a note in a book. 'Go to lunch and then collect these four. The minibus will wait for you and if you don't mind going back by a fairly long route to drop off a few others, you can get them all back by four o'clock.'

'So I won't be coming back here, Sister?' It was a cry for reassurance, a need to know that as yet that terrible man had not spread the news that he was accusing her of helping the students to cheat with their exams. Or was it that he had told Sister that the sly nurse with green eyes was not to have any further contact with anyone in the examination room?

'You will just be in time to go off duty, I expect,' said Sister with a kind smile. 'It can be boring here and you have been a great help.'

'Thank you, Sister.' Clover gulped. That might be the last kind word she received from anyone in her chosen profession. I might never even start work on a ward, she realised with growing dismay. If he tells Matron what he thinks of me, I might never have the chance of proving that I am a girl who can be trusted and who wants with all her heart to be a success.

'Are you quite all right, Nurse?'

'Yes, Sister. I'm a bit tired, that's all. My TAB jabs gave me a bad time and that's why I'm here, on light duty.' It was no longer true that she felt any trace of the headache and discomfort of previous days but she made it her excuse for the sudden tears that threatened to fall.

'Ah, yes, you are Nurse Dylan. I heard that you had been ill. You need some food. Leave the desks and go and find something to eat. Are you having lunch here?'

'It's all right, Sister. I'll do the desks. I'm meeting my cousin for lunch outside the hospital, if that's permitted.' She bit her lip. This was another opportunity for Sister to say that she had heard about the nurse who had tried to help her cousin in his exams, but it was becoming increasingly obvious that the man with furious blue eyes had said nothing to the sister in charge.

He must be someone in authority, she thought. He had such a dynamic presence and seemed to be thoroughly at home in a hospital environment. A man from whom people took orders and a man who could make or break the career of one poor girl. And yet he had said nothing. She recalled the sudden sadness in those penetrating eyes, as if he didn't want to believe ill of her. It might have been wishful thinking on her part, but when it happened, it had been like a friendly touch, trying to tell her something.

'Thank you, Nurse. You have only just come out of PTS, I believe. Good luck with your career. Next to my own training school, Beattie's is the tops.' She laughed. 'You will get used to our awful hang-ups about training schools. It's a great life and I wouldn't change it for anything.'

'And I want to do well, Sister.' She received a very thoughtful look as if she was overstating her enthusiasm. 'I'll tidy the desks and go, if I may.'

Clover went to the first long table that was being used for holding papers and penholders. The wooden stand holding hospital stationery and forms was in a mess, where some clumsy hand had grabbed forms from the middle, scattering the others into an untidy cascade. She sorted them out and neatened the stack. The blotting paper was wet, having been used for mopping up spilled coffee, and she replaced it with new bright blue sheets from a pile on a smaller table. Absentmindedly, she snipped a dead rose from the vase of drooping flowers that did nothing to relieve the general austerity of the room. Noting the lack of water in the vase she went to fill it, and on the way back thought she saw a glimpse of the man in the dark suit, walking away down the corridor. She held back until she was sure that he was gone and then picked up her bag and coat and hurried out to the main gate where Robin paced up and down, looking rather pale and anxious.

'Robin?' she said.

It wasn't easy to talk to him. How could she accuse him of doing what he had not in fact begun to do? After all he had made no mention of why he wanted to see her. She tried to imagine other matters in which he would need her help, but seeing his tense expression, she could form only the same opinion as the man with blue eyes—that her cousin, who had been so honest all his young life that he was almost boring about it, could be so desperate about his own future that he was willing to risk hers.

'Am I glad to see you, Clover!' he said. 'I could hardly believe my eyes when I saw you in there. I couldn't believe my good luck.' He walked beside her, slowly, and looked down at her sad face. 'Or I hope it's my good luck,' he said, with less confidence. 'You don't look overjoyed to see me. Are you cross with me because I spoke to you in front of the great man?'

'What great man?'

He smiled slightly as if she had made a feeble joke. 'I came to the hospital with some papers the Prof had forgotten to bring. I am a bit slack as far as work is concerned at the moment, so I don't mind acting as dogsbody. He rang up in a fury and I rushed over with them. Took my mind off things.'

'You came with papers?' She stopped in the middle of the pavement and a man collided with her, murmuring unflattering things about girls who didn't look where they were going. 'I'm sorry,' she said.

'In here,' said Robin, leading the way into the crowded bar. The too-warm air met them and enfolded them in a waft of delicious smells. 'There's a table over there. Quick, grab two seats,' he said. 'Have you any change? I haven't brought much out with me.' Clover raised her eyebrows. 'I'll pay you back,' he said.

She handed him a note and he went to the bar, leaving her facing the sea of faces, the animated voices and the general air of busy exchange of opinions, humour and laughter. Most of the people were from the hospital and she ached to be allowed to claim a part of this life and to be one of the crowd. She watched her cousin coming back to her, carrying the tray carefully. He set down the glasses of cider and two plates of beef sandwiches surrounded by fresh salad, and in spite of her misery, the resurgence of her usual healthy appetite refused to be ignored.

'It looks good,' she said.

'If you're as hungry as I am, it's a feast,' he said. She saw him take an enormous bite and half close his eyes in ecstasy. 'That saved my life,' he said.

'For someone not given to great enthusiasms about food, you are making a lot of fuss about a very good but not unusual beef sandwich. Or didn't you have breakfast?'

'That's more likely,' he said, grinning for the first time. 'I now know what it is to starve.'

'Robin, I don't want to sound inquisitive or even mildly suspicious, but what are you talking about and why are you so glad to see me?'

'Can you lend me some money?'

'Why?'

'Because, as from three days ago, I haven't had a penny to my name.'

She stared at him in amazement. 'But that's silly. You have a full grant, made up by your doting parents, and I know you have presents of money for birthdays and Christmas. You haven't blown it all on horses?' She viewed him afresh. Could the mild, pleasant boy she had always known, have changed so much? Was there something about living away from home and having to mix with many other types of people that had undermined his basic good sense?

'Good grief, no! What do you take me for?' he said in an aggrieved tone. 'My grant hasn't come through and the authorities are breathing down my neck for my rent. I thought I would pay it in two halves, using this instalment of my grant for the first half, but it just hasn't come. I rang the post office and there was a local strike among postal workers and quite a lot of mail has been delayed. They say it should be here in about a week, but meanwhile I haven't even enough to buy food.'

'Can't you borrow from other students?'

'My friends all seem to be in the same boat, except for John who has to work in a bar to make up his grant. His father refuses to pay up, even though he can afford it.'

'And he has a high enough income to make a full grant from the state impossible for his son?'

'Exactly. It's hard luck on John. In many ways the poorer the family, the better off the under-graduate can be, as the State forks out for the whole lot, but if parents won't pay and the grant is low, it creates real hardship.'

'Is that the only reason you wanted to see me?'

'Yes, that's all. I mean, no, of course not, Clover! It's very good to see you any time. Now we're both in London, we must meet up. You must come to some of our gigs and if I'm invited, I'll come to Beattie's.'

'I didn't mean to sound offended if that was the only reason you could bear to see me,' she said, with a rather watery smile. 'It's just that for one horrid moment I wondered if you were in trouble over exams and wanted some help.'

Robin looked puzzled. 'How could you help me? You know even less than I do at this stage.' He frowned and then went red. 'You aren't suggesting that I might have wanted you to tell me about your patients?'

She nodded. 'You appeared in the doorway looking pale and wan and latched on to me as if I were a life belt.'

'You couldn't think that, Clover! Do I look the type who would cheat, even if I were desperate?' He looked very annoyed and hurt.

'Don't be angry, Robin. It wasn't me. I was accused of telling students about patients by that horrible man you were talking to when I saw you.

Afterwards, he said he intended telling your Prof and the Matron of Beattie's about it.' She choked on a piece of lettuce. 'I don't know what to do, Rob. I haven't even *seen* a bed patient and I'm about to be thrown out.'

'He can't do that. Even Dr Blamine can't do that.'

'Who did you say he is?' She stared at him. 'Did you say he is a doctor?'

'Only *the* authority on diseases of the endocrine glands. He comes to us sometimes to lecture, and at Beattie's he's the greatest. He was examining here, so you were sure to see him. Didn't you meet in one of the cubicles?'

'He came with us in the minibus the first day and I thought he was . . . oh!' She covered her face with her hands, not sure if she was laughing or crying. 'Oh, Robin, first I called him a patient and wondered why he was cross, then I thought he was just a nosy civil servant trying to organise me. I was quite rude to him, I suppose, if I consider the difference in our status.'

'Well, God help you if you meet again! He doesn't suffer fools lightly.'

'You don't have to tell me that. I still bear the scars,' she said, with feeling. She sipped her cider and the bubbles tickled her lips. It was a soft, light touch, like cool butterflies. Like the brief touch of lips that were, for a magic second, healing and kind. And now he hated her and thought her a cheap nobody who would sacrifice the good name of her training school as lightly as one would cast away a withered leaf. He also thought that she dated patients, and it had taken Sister Tutor exactly one day to fix the idea in the minds of her new school that, among the sins that might be committed at Beattie's, *that* was the one most frowned on and strictly forbidden for the good of patient and nurse alike. There isn't much left for him to despise, she thought.

'I'll write you a cheque, but I'll need it back as soon as possible,' she said. She named a sum that she could spare and Robin gave a sigh of relief. 'I can't manage more as I have some of my own expenses. I have a day off tomorrow and if they throw me out, I shall have to buy a rail ticket to Scotland to the aunts, if they'll have me until I can fix something other than nursing.'

'It won't come to that, I promise.'

'What can you do?'

'I'll think of something.' He laughed, trying to cheer her. 'At least with the aunts, you'll be comfortable. I had ideas about begging a few feet of floor space in your room if I was thrown out for non-payment of rent.' He was joking, but a cold shiver went through her as Clover pushed away her plate. 'What did I say now?' he demanded.

'Don't even joke about that,' she said. 'There's one big favour you can do for me. Do you know Alex Smithers?'

'Yes, and what I knew I didn't like much,' said Robin, firmly. 'You aren't going about with him, are you? Really, Clover, you can do better than that.'

'I am not involved with him in any way,' she said, acidly. 'He's hitching down to a concert at Wembley and says he intends coming to Beattie's. I couldn't put him off and he calmly announced that he'll be with me for two nights. Could you put him up in your block? We don't seem to have guest rooms in the nurses' block and students have to leave at midnight or there's a row.'

'Sure. It's the least I can do. As soon as he comes, send him over and tell him to ask for me. If he says he's from university no one will ask too many questions. In Hall, people come and go all the time.'

'Bless you, Robin. That's a load off my mind.' She smiled, and he saw that she was more relaxed. 'Why not come over tomorrow night and take him back with you? I can manage coffee and buns in the sitting room and it will show the others that Alex is not my boyfriend, although he seems to be pushing that idea again,' she said with disgust.

'That might be good. I haven't had much joy with the nurses at our place yet. But perhaps if you were to introduce me to some of your friends . . .'

Clover warmed to him. She knew that under the hard-working exterior was a shy person longing for company but too withdrawn to push himself forward. 'I'd like you to meet Rosalyn. She's fun,' she said.

When they finished the fruit pie and ice cream, they both felt better and far more optimistic. Robin left, clutching the cheque and some small change for the tube, and Clover felt that she had crossed one hurdle. Robin had no exams at present, so even if she was accused of helping him, there was no substance for such accusations and she could hold her head high and refute them.

But the fact that Dr Blamine still had at least two other matters that reflected badly on her ability as a nurse and as a person still hung heavily in her heart. She tried to think that it wasn't important to have his good opinion. I may meet him later after I've been at the Princess Beatrice for a year and am no longer less than the dust before such high-and-mighty individuals, she decided. But there'd be not the slightest risk of having to do anything for him on the wards. He'd want the full attention of Sister, his house physician, his firm of dressers and students and the senior nurses trailing after him as he made his godlike descent on the wards! In the shadows of the sluice room where I belong, I can cower like a hospital Cinderella and hide among the piles of sluiced bed linen, Clover thought with a wicked smile.

Three of the patients were ready for the return trip to Beattie's and the driver was fuming as they waited for the last. Three other men, who had come for treatment with the urological department and were due back at the kidney unit, were sitting in the back seat. As soon as the last patient arrived, the driver started the engine. At that moment a nurse ran to the closed door and waved a large envelope at Clover. The driver mumbled but stopped long enough for Clover to take it.

I suppose I forgot some more notes, she thought,

but she was sure that she had gathered up everything given to her to take back in the minibus. This must be a message for Sister or for the personnel in Outpatients.

She slid the door shut again and saw that the envelope was addressed to her. She turned it over curiously. She didn't want to open it in front of the patients as she had a feeling that in it she might find the ultimate reprimand from Dr Blamine. Why should it be him? She brushed aside the idea. I'm becoming obsessed by him. He's been so horrible that it's going to take several days to get him out of my mind, she reassured herself.

She smiled at one of the women who now looked rather tired. She was reminded of Mrs Street who had been taken into the Princess Beatrice as an in-patient after her morning session in the examination room.

I think I have trouble, but what is it compared with women like her? I have my youth and health and my future before me to plan as I want it, she thought as she stared out of the window at the fast disappearing bridge over the river. What future could there be in London for a girl who didn't fit into the hospital pattern? Many of her friends were engaged to be married, safe in cosy little jobs that put no pressures on them, happy in a certain way that did not reach the heights of achievement or the summit of fulfilment in love. They had happiness enough to make them think that there was nothing more to be taken from life, but could Clover Dylan be content with such an existence after being here, seeing the work that was waiting to be done, meeting people like Dr Blamine?

Why think of him again? She shivered. If I stay here I shall experience more extremes of emotion that I dreamed possible, she thought. The misery of the morning was proof of suffering. A frisson of tremulous sensuality spread over her. I'm being silly, she told herself. Who is there to make me feel like that among the men I shall meet? Alex, with his smooth, pawing approach? Someone like her cousin who did nothing for her libido?

'We're nearly there,' she said to her patients, firmly dismissing the vision of a dark head of hair and dark hairs on the back of a certain man's hands.

The envelope almost burned a hole in her hand as she turned away at last from the bus, and the waiting cars took the remaining men and women to their homes. She slid open the flap and looked inside. Economical, she thought with a shrug. It was short to the point of curtness and behind it she could read his resentment.

'Nurse Dylan,' she read, 'There seems to have been a misunderstanding. Please learn to be more explicit if you have to make excuses to those in authority in future. You could avoid a lot of personal trauma if you did so. I now know that your cousin came to see you about a personal matter, so there will be no further mention made of your behaviour.'

It was signed with a scrawled and almost illegible signature and try as she may, Clover couldn't read the first name. Her relief was mixed with anger. It was his fault not hers that he had jumped to the conclusion that she was being dishonest. Or was it? He had already suspected that she was helping students the first day, and there was the little incident about dating a patient, too. *He's working off his bad temper on me,* she decided. *It would be a pleasure not to see him again.*

It was a relief to know that there was no need to see Matron and she could take her day off tomorrow and enjoy it. Nothing could happen now to threaten her happiness at Beattie's. She tore the note viciously, breaking a finger-nail as she did so. 'Damn!' she said. She put the torn pieces into her bag and went to the ward to report that all patients were safely back or on their way home.

'You are off tomorrow, I believe, Nurse.' Sister was hot and busy and had no time to waste. 'Very well. I hope you are stronger? We are going to be busy when you get back. I have three thyroids waiting for treatment in the sideward and they are at complete rest. It makes for a very busy ward.' Her eagle eyes saw the torn nail. 'Get your nails cut short before you come back on duty, Nurse. Torn nails look slovenly and long nails are forbidden on duty. Off you go, have a good rest and come back fighting fit.'

Her smile took away the sting in the mild reprimand but, as she left the ward, Clover thought ruefully that even the broken nail was due to Dr Blamine. Sister would never have noticed her nails if it hadn't been for his letter! However, she didn't throw away the torn pieces of hospital notepaper but put them carefully in the top drawer with her tights.

The corridor was quiet and she thought there might be enough time to shower before the rest of her set, coming off duty, came chattering along from the main part of the hospital. I need a little time to myself, she thought, hoping that Delia, with her probing eyes, wouldn't be off duty.

As she turned on the cool water and let it slide over the scented soap with which she had covered her body, she heard the telephone ringing downstairs. She turned up the pressure and ignored it, Alex wouldn't be here until tomorrow. Robin wasn't coming until tomorrow evening—and if he had a message for her it could wait until she was dressed. And anyway, it wasn't likely that the call was for her. Her grandmother had said on many occasions that bad news could wait. The caller could ring again if it was important. The ringing stopped and she decided to wash her hair under the shower. The warm water seemed to do more than wash away the surface dust of the city. She revelled in the smoothness of the sweet-smelling shampoo that ran down from her hair over her firm and rounded limbs and wondered if she had enough sun-tan from the early heatwave to let her wear a low-cut dress if she went out to a theatre with Robin.

She smiled as she thought of her cousin. He wasn't the type to turn her on even if they were washed up together on a desert island, but he had his good ideas and one of those had been that they should meet to queue for seats in the gods when there was any programme in the West End that they wanted to see. It would be less lonely to go with someone she knew and his company would put no emotional pressure on her, unlike the same arrangement made with someone like Alex.

'If my grant comes, we'll celebrate,' Robin had said. 'I'll pay you back the money you lent me and we can go to the play at the Adelphi, if you want to see it. I can nip over on the morning of your day off next week and try for tickets at the kiosk in Leicester Square where they sell cut-prices seats to students on the day of the performance. If I can't get any there, I'll get in the queue as soon as I can in the evening and you can join me.'

'If I get there first, I can wait for you,' she said. It had made her realise the value of having a friend close at hand. As she towelled her body and flicked the drips from her soaking hair, she had the uneasy premonition that although it had been Robin who needed her help this time, there might be a time in the future when she would want his shoulder to cry on.

She reached for her clothes and found that she had run along to the shower room wearing only her dressing gown, intent on getting her shower over before others came banging on the door and telling her to hurry. She gave her hair another rub, sending it into a tangle of auburn curls, glistening dark and thick and impossible to keep from falling over her face. The towel was now more wet than her hair, so she went out into the corridor with it swathed over one arm, the other hand holding back her hair and her feet slopping in mules that should have been thrown out long ago as they no longer gave her a firm foothold.

The telephone was ringing again, and the compulsion to answer it was strong. It's nothing to do with me, she told herself, but the insistent tone became a personal challenge. It might not be the same person. Many calls come for nurses, and this might be another boyfriend with a completely different message for another nurse. It's none of my business. The ringing stopped—and now the problem was to know if it had stopped because the caller was tired of trying to get through, or because it had been answered. If it had been answered they'd soon know who the call was for.

'Nurse Dylan?'

Clover clutched the dressing gown tightly round her and knotted the tie belt. 'Coming!' she shouted. She flung her towel into her wash basin so that it wouldn't make anything in the room wet and pushed her hair once more away from her eyes. Oh, for another dry towel! But there wasn't time. If the telephone had been ringing for so long, the caller must by now be rather annoyed with her. It might be Robin, of course, and he'd understand the difficulties of the system.

'Hello,' she said, with a voice husky from effort. Small drips of water sank into the collar of her dressing gown and she slackened the belt slightly so that she could ease the fabric away from the wet hair. The gown slipped to reveal the dimpled shoulders and the fine warm skin, the gentle curve of her throat and the dark shadow that promised the cleavage between firm and uptilted breasts. The telephone was placed in a small office that was no longer used as such but held the mail slots and a table for messages.

'Hi there, remember me?'

Her heart plummetted. 'Not you again, Alex? I didn't expect to hear from you until tomorrow.'

Behind her, the door opened and she was dimly aware that some other person was in the room, no doubt looking for mail or leaving a message for a nurse off duty. There was a notice board on the wall where many scraps of hospital information were posted to tell staff of concerts, free tickets given for various entertainments, the fixtures for hockey and tennis matches, and a darts match at the Falcon, the popular and much patronised pub across the park that Beattie's staff seemed to look on as a private club.

'Not pleased to hear my dulcet tones, darling?'

'No, I'm not very pleased.'

'I thought I'd warn you that I might be here earlier than I thought. I made a mistake about the concert. It's tonight. I hitched down just in time and I'm ringing from a call box before eating and getting into my seat. See you about midnight, or soon after.'

'You can't come here. It isn't allowed and I've been in enough trouble for one day.'

'Tut, tut, not my kind of trouble, I hope.'

The insinuating voice increased her anger. 'Alex,

listen to me. I can't have you here and that's final.
I'll give you another number to ring and you'll have
to ask for Robin Diamond. He's my cousin and he
said that you can sleep in his room. I saw him today
and he told me it would be all right.' She gave him
Robin's number.

'But I don't want to sleep with your cousin,
Sweetie.'

'Well, you can't come here. I'd get turned out if I
had a man in my room all night.'

'I'll ring, but if I can't get him, don't be surprised
if I come to Beattie's tonight.'

'Alex! Please don't be like that. It isn't fair.'

As she put down the silent receiver she clenched
her hands and cast her glance upwards as if to ask
the gods for guidance. In the glass of the wall
cupboard, the door and some of the room was
reflected and she saw a man standing by the table,
picking up something in a package. It looked about
the size of a large box of chocolates or expensive
biscuits. But it wasn't the reflection of the table that
made her gasp. Her own image in the glass showed
a woman with wet hair that made dew drops on her
bare shoulders. She saw the way that her gown had
fallen, making her almost nude from the waist up.

I look like an abandoned harlot, she thought,
with growing shame. How could I forget that this
hostel sometimes has male guests and that some of
the senior staff have rooms here? With a violent
movement, she drew the belt more firmly together
to fasten the front of the gown and stood up,
wriggling her toes back into the mules.

The man in the doorway had a dark jacket slung over one shoulder, as if he found the suit he had worn all day far too restrictive. His dark hair was slightly ruffled, as if a weary or angry hand had run through it, and his tie lay loosely over the arm that held the jacket, as if that, too had been taken off in anger or because he was too hot. Dr Blamine stared at her, taking in every detail of her face and body with the deliberate appraisal of a connoisseur of women. His slight smile was an added degradation and his contempt was mixed with reluctant admiration of what he saw.

For one wild moment, Clover thought that his casual style of dress was one step towards undressing and that she might be the focus of an intention at which she could only guess. 'Oh,' she said, her heart beating faster. 'You!'

'Me again. I seem to have the knack of finding you in embarrassing situations.' His glance raked her body again. 'Or is it embarrassing? From the snippets of conversation I inadvertently overheard, you must be more frustrated than embarrassed.' He hitched the jacket higher over his shoulder and the silk shirt clung to the broad chest, showing the echo of dark hair under it.

'I don't know what you mean,' she retorted.

'I may be mistaken, but from where I'm standing I see a very disappointed woman who can't have her lover here to stay. I suppose that your friends in college told you that life in training would be free and easy, to say the least, and now you discover that the Princess Beatrice still sticks to some of its old-fashioned rules and good practical sense, you have had to tell your boyfriend to stay elsewhere.' The blue eyes were diamond hard and as icy cold.

'It's not true. My cousin offered to put him up because I said I knew I couldn't help. Alex is nothing to me,' she said desperately, willing him to believe her or at least to stop looking at her as if any man might buy her body. 'Alex is a friend of my brother. He doesn't live in London and he's here for only two days. I don't want him here.'

'You seem to have a very convenient family. First, your cousin is persuaded to telephone my consulting room to explain away the unfortunate situation in which you found yourself this morning, and then you lean on your absent brother to get you out of this one.'

His controlled anger was far worse than if he had struck her and she cowered back, almost over-whelmed by the force of his manner and by something she couldn't explain. A bubble of curiosity saved her from making a fool of herself. 'Robin telephoned you?' she asked, surprised.

'I was very impressed. He, at least, seemed to think that you could do no wrong. I should let him keep his illusions, unless you want to lose a very good friend.'

'I told you that I wasn't helping him. You are the one who jumped to that conclusion. I don't have to prove anything to you, Dr Blamine.'

She stood erect, unaware of the effect of the damply clinging dressing-gown and her wild hair, which was now drying slightly in lighter tendrils.

'When I am on duty, I know I shall have to treat you with the respect that your position demands, Dr Blamine, but I would like to say, just once, that I think you are the most detestable man I've ever met and I hope that I never have to work under you.'

He relaxed, the powerful shoulders against the door jamb, a faint smile on the mobile mouth. 'You work on ward ten?'

He sounded almost French. Not for the first time, Clover noticed he had a slight accent when he was angry. 'How did you know?' She frowned. There had been several things he knew about her including the fact that she had been ill. He must have told the sister in charge of the examination clinic unless the busy sister at Beattie's had bothered to do so. He couldn't have been checking up on her, could he? The notion was so ridiculous that it deserved to be forgotten. But it seemed unfair that he knew so much about her while she knew so little about him.

'I didn't ask Robin to tell you,' she said. 'I came back here quite prepared to have my whole future ruined just because you believed what you did, but I would never ask Robin to intercede with you on my behalf.'

'I promise I won't ruin your career. I don't promise that I might not rearrange it slightly, but we'll have to wait and see.'

She distrusted the laughter she now saw in his eyes. His mockery was almost as bad as his searing anger and she lowered her glance.

'Don't you think you should get dressed? I'm not the only man in this building and some might have less control than I have.' He stood aside, listening to the sound of voices coming up to the front door. 'Perhaps if I go first?' he said and walked swiftly to the stairs, reaching them before the outer door opened.

Clover watched him go and pushed her hair from her eyes. On the floor was the silk tie that had lately adorned the neck of the man she most hated, the man who disturbed her more than fury, more than humiliation could do. She picked up the tie and its silver coldness ran between her fingers, making her aware of its owner as positively as a physical touch.

'You're off early. I hope you didn't take all the hot water,' said Delia, her eyes taking in the fact that Clover Dylan was fresh from a bath. Which meant she had been summoned to the telephone in a hurry. 'Who rang you up?' she asked, hopefully.

'A friend,' Clover replied, shortly. Delia looked annoyed. 'Only the man who wanted to stay here. I was hoping to let you meet him tomorrow, but he came a day early,' said Clover with what she hoped was a sweet smile.

Delia looked disappointed. 'Isn't he coming to see you? Is that what he wanted to tell you?'

'I told him to go and stay with my cousin and I hope he does,' said Clover, firmly.

'That's a nice tie. It's a man's tie,' said Delia, her eyes wide. 'He's been here. You're holding out on us, Dylan.'

'Haven't you heard the latest fashion?' said Rosalyn, looking over Delia's shoulder. 'You know. All the very slim smart women now wear men's suits and ties. It will look good on you, Clover,' she said, with a wink that Delia didn't see.

'I'm going to have a bath and then I'm playing darts,' said Delia with the pride of one invited to a royal garden party.

The door closed behind her. 'Poor old Delia, she's thrilled to be asked. And by a man, too! They were short of a darts player and asked a group of us if we played. Delia was the only one who said she could, so they're lumbered with her rather than the pretty little thing they really wanted. However, she means well.' Rosalyn fingered the expensive silk. 'Who *does* it belong to, and why are you standing there as if you had just been struck by lightning?'

'Someone must have dropped it. There was a man in here collecting a parcel while I was on the phone.'

'Like that?' Rosalyn gave a short laugh. 'Sure he wasn't undressing to be in fashion?' Her eyes sparkled. 'That's why you look so crushed. Did he, or didn't he? Is that exhaustion or disappointment I see?'

'You're a fool, Ros,' said Clover, weakly. 'He was on his way upstairs, I think. You do know that some members of staff live here or at least have rooms that they can use?'

Rosalyn put her head on one side and laughed. 'He must be fairly senior to live here and, from the quality of that silk, I'd say he was very well-heeled.'

'Your guess is as good as mine. I didn't notice. I was talking on the telephone with my back to him when he came in. He cast one lecherous glance at me and disappeared in a puff of smoke.'

She tried to sound amused, but her lips were stiff with the effort. 'Honestly, Ros, how can I be expected to know him? I haven't even been on the wards yet, so what chance have I had to meet the medical staff to get to know them?'

And even if I have met one of the most high-powered men at Beattie's, I shall never get to know him, she thought. Is life full of such encounters that throb with something indefinable and leave a girl spent and sad?

CHAPTER FOUR

'MRS Sunderland needs a bed bath and has to have her pulse rate taken before and after each procedure, so you take her pulse and respiration before you even start, and then you take it as soon as the bed is straight again. That way we can see how much effect exertion of any kind has on her,' instructed Sister Scott. 'Do you think you can manage?'

'Oh, yes, Sister.' Nurse Clover Dylan gazed at Sister Scott with sparkling eyes. 'I can't believe that I'm really working on the ward at last.'

'Go on, then, don't stand there all starry-eyed! You make me feel ancient! I can't even recall the day when I went into raptures because I had to do a bed bath.' Sister laughed and seemed pleased with the enthusiasm shown by the new nurse.

The office door opened and a man with very blond hair peeped in. 'Busy, Sister?'

'Yes, very,' said Sister Scott with a frown. 'What do you want, Dr Crown?'

'I only want the names of female patients for the theatre, Sister. Darcy told me there might be three ready soon, so I thought I might get myself known to them.'

Sister smiled. 'I'm sorry I snapped at you, but

you so often come here to waste time chatting up the nurses that I have to be careful.'

Dr Crown gave a lazy laugh. 'I like that. Here I am, giving my valuable time to assist the nurses and you accuse me of having some ulterior purpose, Sister Bridget.' Sister shot him a warning glance. 'Sorry, I forget that on duty we must be very formal for the sake of discipline,' he mocked. 'And what have we here?' He pretended that he had noticed Clover for the first time, although his bold gaze now knew every detail of the neatly dressed trim figure, had a mental note of all her vital statistics and had assessed her as worthy of his notice.

'This is Nurse Dylan, fresh from PTS. She is on her way to do her first bed bath. If you want to see Mrs Sunderland, kindly leave her until last—I want an at-rest pulse rate charted and an after-stress reading.'

He nodded, but his eyes still examined the new nurse. 'Nurse Dylan? Where have I heard that name? Ah, yes, I think there was a package for you, wasn't there?'

'For me? No, Dr Crown. I looked this morning but there was nothing.'

He looked thoughtful, and, Clover thought, disappointed. 'I must have made a mistake,' he said. 'But you *are* the girl who had such a bad reaction to TAB?'

'Yes,' she said, wondering how many more of the staff had heard that shattering news.

'Are you quite better?' He advanced towards her, a soft smile on his lips. 'I think, before she goes on duty, Nurse should have an official clearance, Sister. I think I should examine her glands and if necessary go over her chest.'

'If Nurse Dylan needs an examination, you know very well that she must report to Dr Winifred Manners in the staff clinic,' said Sister, severely. The atmosphere was frosty and Clover began to feel uncomfortable.

'Ah, yes, I'd forgotten all about our hospital routine. But believe me, it would have been a pleasure, Nurse.' He laughed, seeing her blush. 'I'll see you again when you get to the end of the bed bath. I have to talk to Mrs Sunderland.'

The door shut behind him and Clover went as if to follow him out. '*Nurse*,' said Sister. She sat at her desk turning a pen in her fingers. 'Some of the staff make jokes and it doesn't do to take them seriously. Dr Crown, to be blunt, is a man to avoid unless you want your name bandied about. He dates each new and pretty girl who comes here and piles on the charm so that they take him seriously, until another pretty face emerges.' Sister jabbed the pen into a memo pad, ruining at least five pages. 'Maybe I have no right to talk about him like this, but, as you can see, he is very attractive and can sometimes be very, very charming.'

Clover thrust aside the conviction that Sister Bridget Scott had not been immune to the man's charm at some time and still smarted over something. Maybe she had been one pretty face until another had come along? 'He's not likely to make a pass at me, Sister. I'm much too junior.'

'He isn't exactly tied to protocol if the girl's figure is right,' said Sister, dryly. 'Just be careful, Nurse. He means no harm, I like to tell myself, but he's caused a lot of fluttering in this dovecote over the past two years. Off you go and get your patient really comfortable. When you get to the stage when her back has to be done, you'll need someone to help you turn her. Remember, she is at complete rest and must be moved and not asked to move herself. I'll come to help, just to make sure that all is well. Take your time over this one, Nurse Dylan, but not so long that she gets chilled.'

The staff nurse was in the sluice room when Clover went to lay up the tray.

'I know you lay up trays for washing in bed, Nurse,' she said to Clover, 'but for blanket baths it's much better to take a trolley. You can use that one. Lay up all the things you need on the top shelf, such as basin and soap dish, talc and spirit and towels, and have extra blankets ready on the lower shelf to be used for the blanket bath, and the small tray of thermometer and sphygmomanometer and stethoscope in case it's needed. Have everything ready before you go in, so that there is no delay between taking her pulse and doing the bath. While you bath her, ask if she would like to use a bed pan so that she can have one before her back is done and you have help ready to lift her.'

'Yes, Nurse. Who do I get to help me with the bed pan? Sister said she'd help me when I do the back and bed.'

The staff nurse smiled. 'If Sister is there, she will

help with everything needed. We don't suddenly
stop doing that kind of thing for patients as soon as
we wear a staff nurse's or sister's cap!'

To her amazement, Clover felt her own pulse
quickening as she entered the side ward where two
women sat up in bed, wearing very light bedclothes
and thin nightgowns. Mrs Sunderland smiled
weakly at the new nurse, but made no remark as
she saw the thermometer. Clover examined the
level of the mercury with care, hoping that she gave
the impression of knowing what she was doing. She
slipped the bulb under the woman's tongue and as
she took her wrist in her fingers, felt the fine, moist
skin and the tremor that goes with thyro-toxicosis.
The large eyes seemed even larger as they pro-
truded alarmingly, a symptom of the disease. The
pulse rate was rapid and the respirations more than
normal, and Clover carefully noted them on a piece
of paper, having been told that Sister liked to do the
charting, partly to make sure that it was done neatly
and partly so that she would see each entry and be
aware of any changes in the condition of the patient
between her rounds.

The trolley was by the bed and as she pulled the
curtains that separated the beds, Clover was aware
of the woman in the next bed.

'Hello, Nurse!' said Mrs Street feebly. She
looked flushed and very miserable.

'It's Mrs Street, isn't it?' Clover stood by the bed
and looked down at her, shocked by the loss of tone
in the woman's voice, the lack-lustre eyes and the
trembling hands, but she bit back any observation

that might make matters worse. 'I must have a chat with you later,' she said with a smile.

She went back to Mrs Sunderland and covered the bedclothes with a warm fluffy blanket, then took the sheet and bedcover from under it without uncovering the patient, as she had been taught to do in PTS. Mrs Sunderland smiled and seemed to enjoy being washed. She lay still and relaxed and although Clover knew that she was very ill, she wasn't as worried about her as she was about the woman in the next bed.

What could have happened to make her condition deteriorate since the morning in the examination clinic? 'Is that dry?' she asked her patient.

'That's lovely. You've nice firm hands and yet your touch is gentle,' said Mrs Sunderland.

Clover felt as if she'd won an Oscar and blushed slightly. My first bed bath and I haven't killed the patient! She asked her if she wanted a bed pan and the woman nodded. Clover went out to get one, making sure it was warm and could give no shock when put into place. Sister was hovering near the office door and came at once when she saw the new nurse.

'You've been quick,' said Sister Scott. She went into the cubicle, rolling up her sleeves. 'Everything all right, Mrs Sunderland?'

Her practised eyes saw the neat blanket folded back evenly, the trolley in good order and the tidy hair and air of well-being of the patient. She smiled. 'I can see that you are comfortable. Now let's lift you.' In a quiet voice, she told Nurse Dylan what to do and when they had smoothed the drawsheet and the smell of surgical spirit and sweet talcum powder made everything comfortable again, she straightened.

'Good. Now take the pulse again, Nurse. Just wash your hands at the sink and leave the trolley until you have quite finished.' Sister watched the repeat performance of the temperature and respiration and glanced at the note already made.

'Is it all right?' whispered Clover as soon as they left the room. The curtains were still in place and she had to go back to re-fill the water jug and make a note of the fluid consumed, but she had to take the trolley and bed-pan away first.

'She's fine. Her pulse level has settled and this time she seems to show no reaction to being disturbed. Well done, Nurse. I think you can be responsible for her until they take her for operation. Another day without a hectic rise and fall of temperature and pulse rate and she can go to the theatre.'

'If she is so ill, why don't they do it now?'

'Her heart has been working overtime for months. She needed rest and strength to make sure she can stand a fairly long operation and we need to know how she reacts to normal noise and disturbance.' Sister looked at her watch. 'Clear that quickly and tidy the other bed in there. I have to wait for one of the consultants to do his round and he'll want to go in there.'

'Sister? I saw the other patient, Mrs Street, at Bart's, the first morning I was there.'

'Did you, Nurse? Well, have a chat with her later,' she said, a trifle impatiently. 'I haven't time to talk now, Nurse. This *is* a busy ward. Tidy the room and then go for coffee. Report back to me when you come back in twenty minutes.'

She had gone before Clover could tell her how shocked she was to see Mrs Street so changed. I expect she knows, without amateurs like me putting my nose in, she thought and went back to tidy the room. The two women were dozing and Clover crept about, putting things away and making the curtains sit neatly at the head of the beds. She slipped out, half relieved to be un-noticed. It might be difficult to tell Mrs Street that she looked well, when in fact she looked very ill indeed.

Coffee was hot and plentiful and a relief after the tension of working under supervision, even though Sister Scott was very pleasant. But Clover knew that even sisters who had a reputation for being human to their staff would never let any fault go undetected, and it was good to breathe slowly, to sip the scalding brew and to chat to the other nurses who joined her in the cafeteria.

Delia looked hot and bothered. 'What's the matter?' said Rosalyn as she joined them, carrying two cups of coffee. 'Vilma is coming, so I thought I'd save her the time at the counter as she wants to telephone during her break,' she explained. Delia moved up to make room, and sighed with a theatrical upturning of her eyes.

'All right, Delia! We've all noticed that you are bursting to tell us something. Here comes Vilma, so you have a full audience,' said Rosalyn unfeelingly.

'Cow!' said Delia, but didn't seem really annoyed. 'I'm starving.' She took a crumpled and rather greasy bag from under her cloak and began to munch her way through two soggy doughnuts. 'I'll have to cut down soon, but I get weak with hunger after all that hard work.'

'Well, a minute ago, you were bursting with drama. Has the chief paediatrician humbly asked your advice on the running of the childrens' ward?'

'Funny girl!' said Delia. 'I'm just frantically busy, that's all. I had to admit two babies this morning as soon as I went on duty and they are to have operations later today. The rest of the ward is hectic, too,' she said, with an air of generosity. Obviously no one could be as busy as Nurse Delia Norman, but she could admit that some of the others had their busy moments.

'You didn't admit them all on your own, did you?' Clover was impressed. 'I wouldn't know what to do.'

'Hello,' said Vilma. 'Thanks, Ros, that gave me time to put my call through. Hugo may be down today sometime. If he rings and one of you is in the hostel, tell him I'll be there at five. I didn't speak to him this morning, but he had left a message for me to say he would ring me again as soon as he got here.'

'I hope you manage to see him,' said Clover. 'From my experience, messages have a habit of going astray.'

'You mean as it did on your day off?' Rosalyn

giggled. 'Alex had rather a shock to be confronted with Sister in the entrance instead of a welcoming party of nurses, didn't he?'

'Serves him right,' said Clover, with feeling. 'I told him to ring my cousin and go to the place where he lives but he refused to try it.'

'I think he was rather unreasonable to embarrass you like that, Clover,' said Vilma. 'If we hadn't all been there, Sister might have thought you were trying to smuggle him into your room.'

'You were wonderful,' said Clover, with feeling. She recalled the suspicion on the face of the sister in charge of the hostel when Alex arrived at midnight saying that he had been invited to stay there. Vilma had told Sister, calmly, that she knew that arrangements had been made for him to sleep in staff quarters at Guy's and that Clover Dylan had made it clear that she could not receive him as her guest. Alex had been powerless to argue before the placid and confident face of the sweet girl, who was so clearly telling the truth. He had mumbled and apologised, saying he had misunderstood. Vilma had hinted that she was sure that he didn't want to embarrass his friend in any way and asked Sister if he could use the couch in the waiting room in the main block.

'How did you know about that couch?' said Rosalyn.

'Hugo came down when I was in PTS and gave a service in the chapel and they allowed him to sleep there as the guest rooms were full.' Vilma smiled. 'One advantage of having a fiancé in holy orders is that he is accepted as a fairly honest person.'

'Well, he's gone now, I hope. I made it clear that I wanted nothing to do with him and he did spend the next night elsewhere.' Clover finished her coffee. 'I ought to go. The ward is getting busy.' She turned to Vilma again. 'I hope you aren't as busy as Delia. She's been run off her feet, I believe.'

Delia came back from the counter with more coffee.

'Isn't it rather ambitious to admit young babies?' Clover asked mischievously.

'Oh, yes. Sister was most kind.' Vilma beamed. 'She let Delia and me stay when she admitted them. They are very tiny and had to be put in special cots that can be tipped so that they don't inhale saliva or vomit. She handled them so well and the mothers must have gone away saying a prayer of relief.'

Rosalyn lifted a sardonic eyebrow. 'Nice try, Delia,' she said.

Clover saw that tension was about to spring up between the two, so she quickly changed the subject. 'Robin is coming over tonight for coffee and hopes to meet you all. If Alex is still there, he'll come too, but I doubt if he will bother now that he knows he isn't welcome. He may be back in Birmingham by now.'

She went back to the ward, smiling as she thought of Delia and her little endeavours to be noticed. The darts match had not been a great success. Delia had omitted to tell the team that she had not actually played except in the garage at home, where her brother had an old board on one wall and some very basic darts. And yet, Clover was sure that, once she made a success of her work, the pretence would go and Delia would come into her own as a very kind and caring human being, just longing for affection.

'Ah, I'm glad you're back, Nurse Dylan.' The smooth voice made her turn sharply as she went to the door of the office to report back on duty. Through the frosted glass she saw that Sister was not at her desk and as she turned to look for her in the ward, she nearly collided with Dr Crown.

'I'm looking for Sister,' she said, and tried to walk past him to the ward door.

'She's behind the curtains round the end bed,' he said. He smiled and walked beside her and when they reached the ward door, he put out a hand as if to open it for her, but kept the swing door closed, looking down at her with laughter in the blue eyes that were so much less intense than the darker brooding eyes that caused her so much heartache. 'No hurry,' he said. 'She's very busy just now and I'm sure you wouldn't want to interrupt her. We could have a tiny little chat in the clinical room. Not quite time enough for you to tell me your life story, but it would be a beginning.'

'I have to do as I'm told, Dr Crown. Sister told me to report back to her as soon as I returned.'

'Frightened of me?' The smooth voice held undercurrents of sensuality and he put a hand on her bare arm. In spite of her anxiety to get back on duty, she looked up, startled at the effect that his touch had on her. There was no doubting his magnetism, and from the triumphant gleam in his eyes, she knew that he had noticed her sharp intake of breath as his hand caressed her elbow.

'No, I'm much more frightened of Sister,' she said, pulling away.

He allowed her to escape and she heard his soft laughter as the door swung back behind her. In the laughter was a note of victory as if he knew that one round of the siege to win the heart of the new nurse was won.

I mustn't let him attract me, Clover thought. He is one of those men with whom it is easy to be friends, but he's far too attractive to be alone with. A bit like Alex, but far more dangerous. Alex, I can manage, but Dr Richard Crown might be rather harder to control.

The curtains were closely drawn round the bed and it was after considerable hesitation that Nurse Dylan put her head through a gap she made at one side. Sister glanced up and smiled. She was standing by the bed of a patient admitted with vague chest pains and some difficulty in breathing which had yet to be diagnosed. A man in a white coat stood on the other side, his dark head bent over the patient and a stethoscope in his hand. As Nurse Dylan paused in the doorway, the woman in bed coughed and the man applied the instrument to her chest, moving it slowly over the skin and then asking her to take a deep breath.

Sister motioned to the nurse to come in and close the curtains again and Clover stood quite still, finding it was as difficult for her to breathe normally as it was for the woman on the bed.

Dr Blamine straightened. 'May I examine her back, now, Sister?'

The sweet reasonableness of his request came with the kind of smile that most of the nurses at Beattie's would give a half-day off to receive. He patted the hand that lay on the coverlet and Mrs Hurd smiled up at him.

'Nurse Dylan, if you would go that side and help me to ease Mrs Hurd forward, Dr Blamine can examine her.'

Clover slipped past the man who had been a thorn in her flesh since she came to Beattie's—was it only days ago that she had first seen him? Her eyelids were lowered so that there was no need to look at him, to smile or to avoid direct eye contact. She followed Sister in all she did, and Mrs Hurd was lifted forward, resting her head on the shoulder of the new nurse. How frail she is, thought Clover. In PTS, the models used were fairly light and rather floppy and hard to put into a specific position, but this woman was thin and pale and pathetically easy to lift, pathetically lacking in muscle tone and amenable to everything suggested to her.

'That's fine.' The low voice was soothing and inspired confidence, but Clover found it far from calming.

If he hears my heartbeat, he'll think it belongs to the patient, she thought with a flutter of panic. Surely he didn't need a stethoscope to hear the thumping in her breast! But her hands remained steady and her eyes downcast as he leaned slightly against her arm and he bent to listen in again.

He took a long time to finish his examination and when he stood away from the bed his smile was still bright. But Clover found it had altered and was no longer convincing. Mrs Hurd, however, still looked at him as if he was about to perform a miracle and as the two nurses made her comfortable again, she sighed and thanked him as if the cure had already begun.

'You can swish back the curtains, Nurse. Dr Blamine and I shall be in the side ward with Mrs Street. Dr Crown has already had a chat with the patient as he will be giving the anaesthetic when they decide that she is ready for surgery. Please bring me the notes from the office and come in, in case we need a lift again,' said Sister.

'Yes, Sister.' Clover tried to walk away normally, aware of the doctor's eyes following her progress with mild interest and a slightly whimsical expression. How had she dared to be rude to him? In this place, with staff ready to leap to his bidding, he was, as Robin had said, the greatest. How could anyone dare to answer back if he said something to hurt or to insult? In this environment, he had the relaxed confidence of one who knew he was all powerful.

The notes were in a folder and Clover hurried back with them to the side ward. She had said she would be unlikely to see Dr Blamine again and if she did, she was unlikely to be involved with him. How was she to know that Sister encouraged new nurses to take part in consultants' rounds and examinations so that in an emergency they wouldn't stand and gape, scared to move when he asked for something?

'The notes? Good.' A firm hand took them from her and the tips of their fingers touched. Did lightning strike in quiet side wards? This was quite different from the touch of Dr Crown's questing fingers on her arm. That was the awareness of a healthy young woman for a virile man and could lead to physical attraction without depths of feeling on either side. This was more. It was within her alone, she knew, but she wanted to take the hand and smooth the sculptured nails and the slight film of darkness above the wrist.

'Come this side, Nurse,' said Sister, and once more, Clover had to bear the elusive scent of aftershave and male cleanliness. Mrs Street was trembling and had little energy to move or to protest, but Clover knew that she wanted to say something.

'She had that an hour ago,' said Sister in a low voice, pointing to a dose of sedative on the chart.

Dr Blamine frowned as he quickly examined his patient's chest. They lowered her gently and he moved away from the bed.

'Bring the notes, Nurse,' said Sister as they turned to enter her office. Clover went to fetch them, her heart thudding again. Dr Blamine sat on the edge of Sister's desk and as Clover entered the office, he took the notes and read them again, referring back to clinic notes.

'I don't like it,' he said. 'I can't pretend to

understand it, Sister. She was not as bad as this the last time I saw her in clinic and I'm sure that the visit to the examination hall did nothing to upset her, but when they recorded her pulse, it was all over the place. And now she is even worse although she is at complete rest.' He stared hard at Sister and the two women were aware of his arrogance. 'She *is* at complete rest, Sister?' ·

'Of course she is! The two in that room have had exactly the same nursing and you can see the difference. Mrs Sunderland is stable and shows all the benefit she can get from rest and sedatives, while Mrs Street seems to fight rest. Try as I may, I can't convince her that she needs help. Do you think she's frightened so much that she's in a panic?'

'Sister?' Clover pulled at her skirt, crumpling the crisp cotton.

'You can go, Nurse. Help with the beds after the dressing trolley has gone and tell Staff Nurse to lay up an aspiration tray.'

'But Sister,' somehow, she had to tell them her conviction that Mrs Street was unhappy about her home conditions.

'That will do, Nurse. Dr Blamine and I have a lot to discuss and I don't think a nurse of your seniority can help us at this stage.' It was said with a bleak smile, as Sister was smarting under the implied suggestion that her patients were not being cared for as ordered.

Nurse Dylan left, the snappy voice following her and the stern gaze of the consultant impressing her with the fact that, here, she was less than important, with no opinions of her own that she dared to voice.

'Staff Nurse? Sister asked if you would lay up an aspiration tray for her, after the dressings.'

'Damn. I haven't had coffee yet and it will be lunch time before I finish at this rate.'

'What do I do now?'

'Oh, help Nurse in the clinical room. There are several pieces of apparatus that need cleaning. After that, it will be time for drinks. You can give those out, but be careful to consult the list of diets. Two patients are on fluid intake charts. They have red stars on their charts. Enter the amount they've drunk on the slip of paper attached and then measure what goes into the fresh jug.'

The rest of the morning was so busy that it was with a sense of release that Clover heard the sound of lunch trolleys coming along the corridor. She had been told to help hand out the first course and then go to lunch, as she would be on duty for the afternoon. Another evening off was welcome, but at lunch-time, all she wanted to do was to eat and to lie on her bed for an hour. The choice was not hers to make, of course, and she knew that a busy few hours still had to be filled before she could leave the ward for the day.

'I wish I hadn't asked Robin to come over,' she said, with a groan. 'I'll never last out until then. How anyone has any social life in this place is a mystery.'

'You'll get used to it,' said Rosalyn. 'I used to feel like that when I did my stint of Red Cross duty, but after a while, it gets easy. I'm glad I did some cadet nursing as I don't feel as bad as you do.' She smiled. 'Of course, you still feel fragile I expect, after your jabs.'

'No, I've forgotten that. I had a busy morning and I met the man I saw at Bart's. He's obviously a very important man here and of course, I've really blotted my book with him for all time.'

'You imagine it. If it's the man who came to our ward, I could fall for him quite easily.'

'I bet he only smiled at Sister and the patients.'

'True, he didn't seem to notice me. But one day I'll trip up at his feet and then he'll have to notice me,' said Rosalyn.

'No good. It just infuriates him,' said Clover. 'If you want some local talent a little easier to get, there is a man about whom I've been warned, who is very good looking and has a very roving eye.'

'Tell me more. Is he nice, or shall we reserve him for Delia?'

They giggled and Clover felt less tense. If only that man would go away, or at least not come to the ward, she could be happy, working and meeting people and sharing silly jokes with her contemporaries. She described Dr Crown and Rosalyn said she'd look out for him, although there wasn't much chance of meeting handsome anaesthetists in Mens' Medical.

'I think you may see him there. He came into Womens' Medical to have a look at some people being treated in there before they have surgery, so he'll probably come and see the men too. We seem to have a mixture, of people waiting and post-operative cases. There's a list tomorrow, I believe.'

'When I was in hospital, the surgeons were all called Mr Whatever. What is your Dr Blamine? He seems to work in your surgical department and yet he comes to see some of our men. He is called Doctor, isn't he? Does he operate or not?'

Clover thought deeply. 'Someone said that he is a surgeon, but in some countries they call all medics doctor. I think they do in the States.'

'He doesn't look English.'

'Don't you think so?' Clover imagined the dark hair and the deep blue eyes, the full lips and straight nose. 'He could be French or Italian, or partly so,' she said. 'And I've remembered that he's an endocrinologist. Perhaps he specialises in ductless glands and does both medical and surgical care of his pet subject. He came to see two thyroid patients this morning—that is endocrines, isn't it?'

'A bit high-powered for me,' said Rosalyn. 'I know now how ignorant I am and I have a deep suspicion that I shall discover even deeper depths of ignorance as time goes by. There's such a lot to learn,' she said, with a satisfied smile. 'I can't wait to do something more important than bedpans.'

'See you this evening,' said Clover, reluctantly preparing to go back on duty.

'Bedpans and tea, beds and visitors, more bottles and then, bliss, off until tomorrow lunch time,' Rosalyn said. 'Don't be late with that cousin of yours. I'm dying to meet him.'

'Not as glamorous as Dr Crown, but we have to

know our place. Spotty students for us until we have been here for a while,' said Clover.

And who wants spotty students, or even amiable, good-looking men like Robin when there are dynamos of such force, destroying all my feeling for lesser men? thought Clover as she reported back to a fairly chaotic ward and helped with bedpans.

CHAPTER FIVE

'I HAVE time to give you a brief report,' said Sister. 'With a ward full of visitors, it isn't easy to get on with routine and there isn't a lot to do now that everyone has finished tea. If you don't mind missing your tea break now you can make tea on the ward and have it while I go through a few of the cases.' Sister Scott knew that she should have given a lecture as soon as possible to the new nurses and that her regular staff also needed a refresher course about the women in their care.

'What lovely biscuits, Sister.' The junior staff nurse watched wide-eyed as Sister peeled away the seal from a large square box and opened it. Inside was a beautifully set-out selection of very expensive French biscuits. A band of gold ran round the outside of the tin and the bright red pattern of birds was very distinctive. Clover Dylan frowned. Somewhere, she had seen a box like that, or at least had seen that particular pattern. Sister Scott handed the box to each nurse in turn, taking a very thick square confection for herself. Clover took a nutty, finger-shaped piece wrapped in bright green foil and wondered which of the patients was rich enough to give away such quality food.

'Who do we thank for these, Sister?' asked one of the nurses. Clover was still puzzling over the box and had an odd feeling that when she had seen that pattern, it was peeping out of the end of a brown paper bag not quite long enough to cover it completely. Her heart beat faster. That's ridiculous, she told herself. It couldn't be the same box that she saw Dr Blamine taking from the table in the telephone office in the nurses' home. She nibbled her biscuit and tried to listen to what Sister was saying, but there was something more. When she went into the room to answer the telephone, the table had been empty, and yet, when she saw Dr Blamine, he had the parcel in his hands, having taken it from the middle of the table.

'Nurse Dylan?'

'Yes, Sister.' Clover gave her full attention to the lecture.

'It might help you if you jotted down a few notes. Later I shall discourage notes, but at first it helps you to learn the names and disorders from which the patients are suffering. Now, we tend to have a lot of diseases of the endocrine system with us at present, because Dr Blamine, who is also a surgeon but likes to be called Doctor, is making a study of this subject. Much of his research has been done in Quebec and America, where he qualified and his expertise is invaluable to us here.'

That explains a lot, thought Clover. The dark hair, the arrogant, handsome head and the piercing blue eyes.

'Oh, you wanted to know who sent the biscuits? It was quite unexpected. I had no idea that he thought so highly of us,' said Sister with a pleased smile. 'He was a little put out the other day and I think that this is a peace offering. It was Dr Blamine, of course. I can't think of anyone who would bring us such a lovely gift.'

The tap on the door was rhythmic as if the person outside was on very intimate terms with Sister. A head came round the door before she could say anything and Dr Crown came into the room.

'Don't let me disturb you, Sister. Carry on, and yes, I will have a cup of tea if you press me.' He grinned and a ripple of giggles ran round the small office.

'You can have a cup of tea and stay if you promise to be quiet. I might be glad to ask you to explain a snatch, to the nurses—so don't think you can descend on us without working for your tea,' said Sister Scott. 'Have one of these, they're delicious.'

He reached across and took a cream-filled brandy snap wrapped in silver. Looking straight at Clover, he said, 'How good of the recipient to share with the rest of you. If I had these given to me, I'm afraid I wouldn't be so public-spirited.' For no reason that she could think of, Clover blushed.

'Oh, these are for all of us. Dr Blamine brought them to the office himself. He was hovering about as if looking for someone to take them from him. I asked, in fun, if they were for me, and he said it might be an idea if the whole of the staff shared them.'

'No nice card with it?'

Clover knew that Dr Crown was looking at her

again, but she pretended not to notice and searched for a tissue in her pocket with which to wipe her sticky fingers.

'No, and it wasn't even wrapped very well.' So the parcel was the same one. It couldn't have come through the post in that condition, so he couldn't have collected it from the post-box or from the lodge—unless Claude had taken to unpacking parcels as well as holding letters up to the light to see the contents. And even the nosy porter in the lodge wouldn't get away with that.

Dr Crown handed round the box again, pausing when he came to Clover and telling her to take two. 'That's not fair,' she said.

'But you've been ill and I'm sure that Darcy would like to think that you had your full share.' She took one and waved away the offer of more.

'I must get on,' said Sister. 'Now you have all seen Mrs Sunderland?' There was a murmur of assent. 'She is a very bad case of neglected thyrotoxicosis. Some patients carry on for years taking drugs to combat the disorder and manage very well, but there are some who cannot be controlled sufficiently, and they have to have a large proportion of the thyroid gland removed.' She turned to Clover. 'Did you cover that in your anatomy?'

'Yes, Sister. The thyroid is situated at the base of the throat, lying on either side of the larynx.'

'Good. It gives out a substance called thyroxine which steps up the basal metabolic rate, burning up calories and making the patient ever-hungry, but losing weight. That is, if it is being produced in excess of body needs. As the burning up rate increases, so does the pulse rate, the activity of sweat glands, and the hands develop a tremor. Do you understand?'

'And Mrs Sunderland had popping eyes, too, Sister,' said a nurse.

'Yes, that is a symptom, too. They are very nervous and that is why we have them in as in-patients to let them settle down before surgery.'

'Aren't they scared of the operation? That would send my pulse rate up if I had the condition,' ventured the next up in line from the new nurse.

'Ah, that's where we are very cunning.' They all turned to Richard Crown who leaned indolently against the desk. 'Every day, we talk to them and I examine them as if it is routine. They have a mild sedative by injection at the same time each day and it becomes routine also. They know that we are waiting until they are really fit and they think they have loads of time to lie around being spoiled, which is very nice if you have such pretty nurses to care for you.' He grinned. 'This lot is wasted on a female ward, Sister, as I keep telling you.'

He held his hand up as if to prevent the storm of protest and continued. 'One day, when the pulse rate is level and the chart isn't doing silly things, we give a dose of pre-medication instead of the usual weak substance. They are on cloud nine before they know what is happening. Only then do we undress them and put them in a theatre gown, and eureka! The patient wakes up with a heavily bandaged throat, a sore feeling and is well on the way to recovery.'

'Is that the time? I'm afraid we must leave the others until later,' said Sister.

'But Sister, Mrs Street,' began Clover.

'She is the same, only we can't seem to get her stabilised. She will have to stay in for some time, I'm afraid. I asked her to tell her sons when they come to see her that she will need more nighties if she is to wear her own in here.'

'But Sister . . .' said Clover.

'I think you'd better begin bedpans with the junior staff nurse, and then do the backs in the side ward with her.'

Sister went away to talk to any of the visitors needing to see her about their relatives. Richard Crown touched Clover's shoulder and she turned to find that they were the last to leave the office. She tried to pass him.

'Off this evening?' She stared at him, unwilling to tell him. He glanced at the off duty rota on the wall and smiled. 'Nurse Dylan, off from five p.m. Tomorrow, off in the morning and back to Sister Tutor in the afternoon, ward for the evening. That's no good to me as we have a list, but even the busiest anaesthetist needs a drink after duty and I shall take you to the Falcon tomorrow evening at nine.'

'I can't,' she began.

'I think your hair is just right the way it is now.' He smiled and the glance he gave her was almost a caress.

'My hair?' She put a hand to it but found it sleek and controlled under the tiny cap.

'Isn't that the usual excuse for a tactful brush-off? Hairwashing? Or do you write letters home to deepest Hampshire or wherever it is? Do you have fifteen cousins to whom you write a four page letter every week?'

She laughed. It was impossible not to like him. Sister must be prejudiced. He was harmless and good fun. 'Poor man, do you often get turned down?'

'Not often,' he said, his eyes narrowing slightly.

'I have to go out this evening with my cousin, so I should stay in to study, tomorrow. Really! I do have to study.'

'Then I shall help you. Did you like my little talk? I am the answer to a studying nurse's prayer.' She shook her head but with less conviction. 'Please, just a drink, and I promise that there will be no strings attached.' She gave him a searching glance but his eyes were free of guile and his whole attitude told her that he was just a nice guy who wanted her company for part of an evening.

'All right. Just an hour, then.'

'I feel honoured,' he said. 'Anyone who comes out with me after rejecting a gift from the most sought-after man at Beattie's is paying me a real compliment.'

'What do you mean?'

'I adore those green eyes when you look surprised and so refreshingly innocent. Did I say no strings? Ah, well, perhaps the softest of silk threads.' He waved playfully as he left the ward.

'Nurse? Sister said you were to help me. Come on, we haven't long if we are to go off duty. I'm off, too, you know and I want to get away.' The aggrieved voice of the junior staff nurse called Clover back to reality. What on earth did Dr Crown mean? What present? Who was the most sought-after man at Beattie's? Her heart beat faster. If she had to name him there could be only one man, the handsome French Canadian with the dark curling hair and dark blue eyes. She smiled as they made beds, imagining him among the tall fir trees of Canada, perhaps wearing a red check shirt, rolled up at the elbows, showing the strength and muscles of the workmanlike hands, the fine dark hairs on his arms.

'Are you all right? For goodness' sake stop dreaming. If it's Tricky Richard you fancy, forget it. He's had most of the cream in this place at some time and is hungry for more, but it doesn't mean a thing.' The note of dislike made Clover think that this was another conquest on his list.

'I can always say I want to wash my hair,' she said, and made a perfect mitred corner to the blanket.

'Just the side ward now. Better get a bed pan for Mrs Street so that she is disturbed as little as possible.' As Clover went to get it, she saw the door of the side ward open and the staff nurse pointing down the corridor to the public telephone. A man who must have been visiting Mrs Street hurried away and when Clover came back to the room, there were no visitors there. Mrs Street looked flushed and exhausted. The nurse was taking her pulse and frowned. 'You've been talking for too long. I think I'll have to tell your son to come back tomorrow.'

'He won't help me,' the woman said, in a broken voice. 'I must go home, Nurse. I am needed there. I have nobody I can depend on.'

'I know you must be upset, Mrs Street, but this nervousness is a part of your condition. It will go as soon as you have that nasty piece of gland out and can relax.' She smiled. 'You need rest and we can't do anything until you rest completely.'

'You don't understand. My son won't help me and I have to go home to him.'

The nurse raised her eyebrows and went out to find Sister. 'I'll get her a sedative now. I think she's rambling. You do her water jug and talk to her, but don't make her talk.'

The woman put a shaking hand on Clover's wrist. 'You know what I mean, Nurse.'

'You have a husband who is ill?' Mrs Street nodded. 'Haven't you told anyone?'

'What's the use? My son isn't his son. He doesn't understand. He told Sister that everything is fine at home and he thinks my husband, his step-father, can manage, but he can't.'

'What's wrong with him?'

'I've never told my son what the trouble is. He thinks it's a nervous condition and he's for ever saying he should pull himself together. I hide the bad times from him, but when my husband forgets to take his drugs, he's a schizophrenic. If I'm not there, he'll forget his tablets and he'll end up back in that hospital.' Her shoulders shook and she wept, openly. 'I have to get home, Nurse.' She swung her legs over the edge of the bed.

'No, Mrs Street, you mustn't. You'll make yourself very ill if you do that.' For a few moments, the woman seemed to find terrific strength from somewhere and she pushed against the girl and sent her reeling away from the bed.

'I'll explain and they will do something. I *promise* you, they'll do something. Oh, where is Nurse? Where is Sister?' Clover tried to sound comforting despite her panic. She rang the bell and tried to get Mrs Street back in bed. 'You must stay, Mrs Street. I promise I'll tell them.'

'*Merde! qu'est que c'est que ca?*' The enraged blue eyes flashed as Dr Blamine picked up the patient bodily and with surprising control and gentleness, considering his shocked anger, popped her into bed and sat firmly on the edge so that she couldn't move. 'Oh, *no!* Not you again?'

'Dr Blamine, you must listen to me.'

'And what delightful excuse is it this time? You do know that this lady is at bed rest? I see that you do.'

'Please, Doctor. It isn't Nurse's fault. I was trying to get out to go home. She tried to stop me.'

'Is that so? And are we such terrible people that you find us . . . insupportable?' The slight French accent was coming through and if Clover had been less scared, she would have revelled in the sound.

'She wants to go home because her husband at home is ill.'

The blue eyes lost a little of their fire, but the storm was still raging. 'And why does that make her want to risk her life? Someone is caring for him, aren't they? You wish to be well so that you can help him back to health, don't you, Mrs Street? If you are ill, too, then only relatives and neighbours and of course the social services can help.'

'But that's what I've been trying to tell everyone since Mrs Street was admitted, but *nobody would listen*.' Clover's anger made her shout and the room seemed to echo with her cry. 'Everyone said shut up, or words to that effect, treating me more like an infant than a responsible woman trying to learn an exacting job.'

Mrs Street sensed that the battle was being fought for her and closed her eyes. The surgeon put a hand on her pulse and kept it there. 'Well?' he said, his voice icy and calm. 'I'm listening.'

Clover told him all that she had learned from Mrs Street, beginning at the meeting in the minibus. 'I didn't know what was wrong with her husband, but from the way she mentioned it I knew it was something that she couldn't discuss with anyone. And now, knowing that she has never told her son the full extent of his condition, it seems clear that home helps and the social services haven't been told that Mr Street needs supervision.'

She gasped for breath. It had come pouring out as if she thought that Dr Blamine would stop her, but when she ventured to look at him directly, his eyes held a kind of tenderness and amusement that she had always reserved for pets of a particularly fluffy type. He slowly left the bedside and came towards her.

She was rooted to the spot while Mrs Street, who had opened one eye to see what was happening, gaped as she saw the handsome surgeon gather the pretty nurse into his arms.

'*Tu es fou,*' he said. '*Mais je t'aime.*' He swung her high and then let her down, gently, placed a smacking kiss on each cheek and looked into her eyes. He seemed to like what he saw and a hint of mischief warmed the blue depths as he kissed her full on the mouth. 'An old French Canadian custom,' he told an amazed Mrs Street.

'Well!' was all that Clover could find in her vocabulary.

'Very well! Now we can make progress.' He sat on the bed once more. 'We will make a bargain, you and I,' he said to Mrs Street, gently. '*You* stay with us and be helped back to health and *I* promise that within an hour, someone will be with your husband, assessing what is needed.' He looked at the notes fixed to the chart. 'I see that we have the address of your own doctor and of a neighbour. The social worker will send someone to talk to your husband and if it is necessary, he can be sent to a convalescent home that is very pleasant and to which you will be sent for your recovery after the operation. You can be there together and he will be safe.'

Silent tears fell as Mrs Street pressed his hand between both of hers. 'I'll do everything you tell me, Doctor,' she said.

The door opened and Sister came into the room. 'I thought I saw you arrive, Dr Blamine. Is everything all right?'

'Fine, Sister Scott. Mrs Street has explained why she has not been responding to treatment, your capable nurse has stopped her patient escaping and I have to get in touch with the health visitor and whoever else is necessary for this lady's peace of mind. I would like your help, Sister, as I know very little about the formalities of this in Britain. Perhaps Nurse Dylan should listen as this is useful information.'

'Nurse Dylan is due off duty. You may go, Nurse.' Darcy Blamine watched her leave, a wry smile on his lips. 'Thank you, Sister,' said Clover, demurely. 'Goodnight, Mrs Street.' She knew that Sister Scott was watching her and she decided to ignore the man who seemed to fill the room with his charisma.

Her lips were slightly bruised and she touched her mouth tenderly. The hurt wasn't important, but what of the trauma suffered by her heart? His arms had been around her and she had felt the hardness of his embrace. It had been a light-hearted show of exuberance from him because he had at last solved a puzzle that had worried him. If Sister had been there she would have suffered the same treatment, Clover knew, and the thought gave her no pleasure. Were all the men at Beattie's like that? She smiled. I'll have to be careful when I go out with Richard Crown, she thought. But it would have been nice to believe that the kiss had been for her and her alone, and not for just any woman who happened to be there.

The door of the nurses' home was propped open and the evening light was golden across the polished wooden floor. A bird singing in a tree made Clover look up and laugh softly. I can't complain that life is boring, now, she thought and went in, dragging her cap from her head to relieve the tension of a white headed cap pin too tightly jabbed into her hair. A shabby rucksack leaned drunkenly against the table in the hall, the frayed sleeping bag poking out from its restraining straps and the bulges in the side pockets fighting the zip fasteners. Clover eyed it with deep suspicion. It might not be anything to do with Alex, but to her it screamed of him. Her mood darkened. I hoped he was gone, she thought and then heard laughter from the kitchen.

Rosalyn was sitting on the mahogany table that did duty as a dining table, a desk for those trying to study—even if they paid more attention to the gossip around them than the books they were supposed to be reading—and a place for those who had failed their exams to collapse and weep in misery while being plied with strong coffee by their more successful friends. Rosalyn was showing a lot of very desirable leg, clad in sheer black tights and she swung the shapely pins for the benefit of Alex, who sat where the view was very good. He barely looked

up when Clover greeted him. 'Coffee or tea, anyone?' she asked.

Rosalyn paused in the middle of a highly-
coloured account of her first day on the wards, to
nod and laugh. 'Tea, if you're making it,' she said.

'Coffee,' said Alex.

'Tea,' said Clover, firmly. 'I only make one or the
other.'

'Any biscuits?' said Rosalyn.

'No. I wish I'd scrounged a few of the ones we
had on the ward. Dr Blamine gave them to Sister to
divide and some of the others took several away off
duty.'

'Sure you haven't any?'

'Quite sure, Ros. Why?'

'Oh, nothing.' Rosalyn stopped swinging her
legs. 'I'll come and look in the cupboard. I might
have some in my tin.' As soon as they were in the
area away from the table, Rosalyn turned. 'Richard
Crown seemed to think that you had a whole box
given you by a very distinguished person.'

'Me? I only shared the ones he sent to the ward.
Even Sister was surprised to get them.'

'Dr Crown said that he saw Dr Blamine with a
box coming here to give them to you as a peace
offering because he had misjudged you in some
way.'

'I haven't had any. He must have changed his
mind. I seem to have the ability to make him mad at
least three times a day.' Clover frowned. 'He did
come in here when I answered the telephone, but
he took one look and went again.' She blushed as

she recalled her appearance that night, and her conversation with Alex on the telephone. 'I think he finds me a loose woman.' She tried to sound as if it was a joke.

'I found this on the floor.' Rosalyn handed her a small card on which the name of the chocolate manufacturers was stamped, leaving space for a short message if a gift was to be given. On it was her name and the words, *An apology, DB*.

Clover stared at the card. He had come in with a parcel, and the box had the same distinguishing marks as the one on the ward. Had he been so disgusted with what he saw and heard that he couldn't bring himself to apologise and certainly wouldn't want to make her a gift of anything but his displeasure?

'He must have changed his mind. Probably thought it beneath his dignity to say he was sorry, and took them to Sister Scott.' She tried to sound casual, but her pulse thumped painfully. How he must dislike her to do a thing like that. Even the sudden embrace, though meaningless as far as feelings were concerned, now took on a more cynical overtone. He was mocking her and letting her know that girls like her were ten a penny and could be picked up, kissed, discarded and forgotten. 'Not a very nice man, as far as I have found. French-Canadian and probably has a chip on his shoulder about other countries . . . or something.' It sounded so weak, like a feeble attempt to strike him from across a room.

Rosalyn giggled. 'Dr Crown said that when Dr

Blamine is excited or moved, he speaks in French.'

'I've heard him say *merde*, which I believe is a bad word, isn't it?' Clover poured boiling water over the tea leaves in the pot. And I bet you'd like to know what more he said, even if it was half insulting, she thought to herself. He had used the very familiar form of address, the familiar *tu*. Had he really said he loved her? It had registered that he had said she was a fool, but had she imagined the rest?

'I think I have some chocolate upstairs. I'll get that,' said Clover, and when she was looking for it in her room she spared time to wonder how it was that Dr Crown and Rosalyn had been discussing her. He works fast, she thought with a smile. I wonder which evening Ros is dating him?

When she reappeared downstairs, Delia had arrived and was calmly drinking the tea that Clover had poured out for herself. She was telling Alex how much she loved playing darts and he was obviously about to be asked if he played. 'If we're going to the local, we can all play,' he said.

'Thanks a lot,' said Clover dryly. 'Count me out.' She poured another cup of tea. 'Where is Robin?'

'We can go on. We needn't wait for him,' said Alex, airily.

'You do as you like. I have an appointment with my cousin this evening,' she said. 'Isn't it time you found your way back up the motorway?'

'Tomorrow,' he said. 'I should be back today but I shall say I had to sit with a sick friend.' He grinned

happily, knowing that, as yet. Rosalyn thought he
was very attractive.

'I'm going up to change. If Robin comes let me
know, Delia.' Clover smiled sweetly. 'Come on,
Ros. Time to put on your war-paint, even if it's
wasted on morons. I see that Delia is the only one
changed, so she can entertain you, Alex.' He made
a half-movement to rise from his seat but the
warning was clear and he saw that his friend was in
no mood for his type of humour or for his company.
He sat down with a sigh and Delia, delighted to be
alone with a very good-looking boy, launched into
her life story.

'He's nice,' said Rosalyn with a reproachful
glance at Clover.

'Some people like snakes,' said Clover. 'I'm
taking my time. If you want to go on with Alex,
that's up to you. I shall wait for Robin and come on
later, if he arrives here at all.' She closed the door
and looked for something to wear. It would be a
very warm evening if the last two nights were a fair
example. She selected a silky dress of amber with
tiny yellow sprigs of flowers. It was a simple style
with a low square neck and tiny cap sleeves. She
rubbed scented cream into her legs and wore no
tights. It was good to wriggle her toes freely in
high-heeled sandals and she found the buttercream
coloured handbag that matched the shoes. After
such a busy day she would have liked to wash her
hair, but she knew it would take a long time to dry
unless she went down to the utility room where
there was a hair drier. And I'm not going on view

again looking like a savage, she thought, tearing at her hair with a hard brush until it shone and curled up with static. She was applying mascara when there was a sound at the door.

'Delia?' she said, thinking that Robin might be downstairs. The door opened and Alex strolled in. 'Get out,' she said, firmly. She ignored him and outlined her mouth with a new lipstick she had bought to pick up the amber tints of the dress. It looked good and if Alex hadn't been staring at her she would have taken longer over it, blotting it with the tiny tissues she kept for that purpose and making sure that she was not too dewy, as she thought of it when there was a faintly gooey layer of lip cover. Alex made no sound but she knew that he was close behind her. 'Get lost,' she said as she put down the lipstick. Still he made no sound and she turned, wondering if she had been mistaken and that he had left the room.

His arms came round her in a vice-like grip that had no gentleness, no welcome firmness. His mouth came down on hers in a kiss in which there was lust and urgency mixed with the need for revenge for every slight she had given him. She struggled and tried to kick him, but the sandals were open-toed and fragile. Her cries of rage were muffled and from outside the half-open door could easily have been mistaken for murmurs of passion as Alex tried to unzip her dress. His hands seemed to be everywhere at once. The chair on which she had been sitting by the dressing table slid from under her and the force pushed him back. As he staggered, she made for the open door and stood by the doorway, her breast heaving with rage and effort, her back to the stairway at the end of the row of rooms.

Alex came out of the room, his hair on end and his shirt untucked. Across his face was a smear of bright lipcolour and Clover knew that her lipstick was badly smudged. 'Get out and don't you dare show your face here again,' she whispered. He gave her a furious look and almost ran for the stairs. Clover heard a hurried remark, possibly of apology as one human being collided with another and turned to see Alex disappearing and Dr Darcy Blamine standing a few yards away from her holding a spray of yellow roses.

He gazed at her in utter disbelief for a second and then the blaze of fury with which she was becoming only too familiar spread over him like a cloud. He handed her the spray, made a curiously formal and graceful bow and stood back. 'At least they match what's left of your lipstick. I suppose that was another of your cousins?' The sarcasm was biting and she went back inside her room to hide her tears, still clutching the gift that had been meant to say thank you, but which now could do nothing but put them light years apart.

CHAPTER SIX

'SURE you're all right?' Robin sounded concerned and Clover was glad that her cousin couldn't see her. The telephone line was bad and any irregularity in her voice could be put down to the defect. He couldn't tell that her eyes were swollen with weeping and her face was tense and white.

Last night she had managed a kind of brittle humour, passing off Alex's behaviour as just something to be expected from him. Even Rosalyn was shattered when she came out of her room and saw the state in which Clover was left after his onslaught. What she didn't know, however, was that Clover could have coped with Alex, and even managed to laugh at him once she had repaired her make-up and zipped up her dress again, but for the fact that Darcy Blamine had once more surprised her at one of the most embarrassing moments in her life. That had turned her cynical laughter to hysteria. Ros had taken the spray of yellow roses from her hand, pushed her back into her room, given her a glass of water and stood over her while she washed her face and returned to near normal.

'You were brave to come out with us at all, but I thought you looked a bit bushed when we came back. I wondered if you had a reaction this morning.'

'You are the nicest man I know,' said Clover, with feeling. 'I don't know what I would have done without you, last night. It was a good idea to go for a walk in the park and to come back for coffee later. Delia could see that she wasn't wanted and Ros had time to calm down. I think she was far more upset about Alex than I was.' Gradually, now that she could talk about it again, she brightened. 'I was sorry for her. She rather fancied Alex and now she wouldn't touch him with a ten-foot pole.'

'I'm glad about that. Give me a ring when you decide that you can face a blind date and I'll fix something for you and Ros. She's quite a girl.'

In spite of her own problems, Clover smiled. Robin and Ros? It could be good, and she made a mental note to push them together at the earliest opportunity. 'I have to go now. I have a lecture this afternoon and I'm on duty this evening. I hope that we're busy so that I have no time to get depressed.'

'Just forget him, and look ahead. I don't think he'll show up here again and in a way it's good to know that, isn't it? I haven't forgotten that I owe you and I'll be in touch as soon as I'm solvent again.'

''Bye, Robin, and thank you.' She went upstairs again, bathed her eyes and put skin freshener on the now less swollen lids. Dear old Robin. He had given her courage. There were still men in the world who were caring, decent and lacking in histrionics. She couldn't recall a time when Robin had lost his cool unless it was justified.

She had half an hour before lunch and wandered

round her room, tidying in a half hearted manner. The sprays of yellow roses were in a tooth mug where Ros had left them, and Clover touched one of the buds that was just breaking through with a shaft of gold like a shy sunbeam. They were choice blooms and faintly scented like the old tea roses that she remembered from cottage gardens in the rain. Delicate flowers, to say thank you for helping him to know what was worrying his very sick patient. Another of the nearly-given presents, spoiled by something entirely outside her control. She shrugged. If he was in the theatre today, the likelihood of seeing him was remote and she could put all her thoughts and energy into doing the work for which she had come to Beattie's.

There was beef stew for lunch with quite good mashed potato and carrots. It was hot and savoury and satisfying and she found that she was hungry. That wasn't surprising as she had stayed in bed until ten and not bothered with breakfast, making coffee on the kitchen hot plate and eating nothing before lunch. After lunch she went to the lecture room for the refresher in the finer points of routine—and what was more important, the chance to ask Sister Tutor about anything that had happened on the wards during the first days on duty.

Gradually the class-room filled and Clover found that everyone but her seemed to have twenty questions to ask. Sister Tutor held up a hand at last and smiled. 'At least you all seem very keen and now I hope you know why I bullied you into all that work. Admit it! It all came in useful, didn't it?'

'Yes, Sister,' said Vilma. 'And everything we found so difficult at first in the practical classes became almost second nature.' There was a buzz of assent.

'Is anyone unhappy with the work or with the ward on which you are working?' She looked directly at Clover. 'Nurse Dylan, you seem very quiet. Are you still feeling unwell?'

'I'm fine, Sister. I get a little tired, but I know I shall enjoy my work. I haven't been on the ward as much as the others, so I haven't had a chance to show what I can do or to get to know the patients.'

'Ah, yes, I was forgetting.' Sister dismissed the thought that Nurse Dylan appeared to be thoroughly miserable and went on to talk about behaviour off duty and the need to talk of nothing to do with the hospital when they were in local shops and restaurants. 'You never know who is listening. The man behind the bar at the Falcon might be worrying over a relative in your ward, and if you make a flippant remark or indulge in a snap diagnosis, even if the case has been puzzling all the highly qualified medical staff, he might get the wrong impression,' she said, dryly. There was a ripple of laughter, but the point was taken.

They all clustered round a long table in the cafeteria for tea before reporting back to their various departments. Clover dreaded her return to the ward and hung back in the corridor as the nurses gradually filtered off to their own wards. She went up the stairs and along the silent and highly-polished corridor. The smell of Beattie's would remain with her for the rest of her life, even if she had to leave soon.

The view from the window was of trees, trying valiantly to defeat the grime of the city, and she wondered why birds bothered to come to the dust and lead-filled air of a big town. Why do any of us come? Why do people work here, live here, love here? A clothes line down the road in the next residential block flaunted a line of snowy white nappies, a couple of pairs of bright blue Y-fronts and two frilly nighties in sugar pink. Clover imagined the young family they belonged to—two people in love and the product of their love! Was the baby crying at the moment, or lying in a pram in the sunshine?

When Clover arrived in Womens' Medical, Sister Scott had her sleeves rolled up and looked as if she would be working in the ward for hours. Clover found her brisk manner catching and hurried to do as she was told.

'We've had three theatre cases today, Nurse. We've also had four admissions and some are for tests tomorrow. I rather think you'll have to stay a bit late tonight. Once the night staff are here, I ought to give a full report as there have been so many changes today.' She frowned. 'Dr Blamine is a very skilled doctor and surgeon and I welcome many of his ideas, but he seems to be changing my department from a purely surgical ward to a centre for endocrinology. True, there are beds reserved for Sir Horace, or rather for his successor. I can never get used to the fact that he has gone and another gynae consultant is here in his place.'

'I saw him at the examinations.' Clover smiled.

'Poor lads who get him! He leads them an awful dance, and half the time he's laughing but they are too scared to know it. However, we have an admission of a woman who is in for investigation of a possible Cushing's syndrome. Her name is Miss Vicary and she is in the end bed. She has to give a specimen of urine when you give out bedpans. I argued with Dr Blamine over that case. She is medical as far as I am concerned, as I don't think it likely that she will go to theatre. Get on with it, then, Nurse. I can't stand here talking all day,' she ended sharply, making Clover jump.

As Sister Scott talked of Dr Blamine she frowned as if the meeting had been stormy. He's bad-tempered and inflexible with Sister as well as the junior nurses, Clover thought, but the news did nothing to cheer her.

It was a feat of some skill to balance Miss Vicary on a bedpan. In theory, she was mobile and able to help herself, but it was really a matter of trying to fit a very large lady onto a normal sized receptacle. Clover was rather puzzled. She had no idea what Cushing's syndrome was and didn't like to ask her patient what was wrong as she knew that the average patient took it for granted that anyone in uniform knew all about them.

Miss Vicary obliged with the specimen after many grunts and groans and was allowed to go to the bathroom to wash before supper, to the relief of patient and nurse alike. She walked slowly, her thick waist bursting through the opening of the hospital dressing-gown which she wore. Her hair was thin and spiky and there was a line of dark hair on her upper lip. The voice that issued from the small mouth was deep and Clover wondered vaguely about sex changes. A quick glance at the chart showed that she was only in her early thirties and yet she looked at least fifty or sixty years of age.

There was no time to wonder. The round was finished, the sluice cleared and bedpans sterilised, as Sister still preferred to use the stainless steel pans and not the disposable variety that didn't always stand up to pressures like Miss Vicary. The junior staff nurse gave out medicines, going to Sister with dangerous drugs for checking before giving them to the patients, and Clover and another nurse tidied beds, gave out drinks and served suppers under the vigilant eyes of Sister Scott.

From the end of the ward came a faint smell of anaesthetics and three still forms, each with an intravenous bottle supported on a stand at the head of the bed, lay sleeping after the morning session in theatre. Clover peeped at the notes when she had a moment to spare and then looked more carefully at one of the sleeping women. It was Mrs Sunderland, lying peacefully without a tremor in her hands, her neck swathed in thick dressings under a neat bandage and looking quite a good colour. Already, her pulse rate was down much further than at any time since admission.

In passing, Sister said, 'Dr Crown gives a very good anaesthetic. Recovery said that none of these were sick.' She laughed. 'I think he hypnotises them with charm, and doesn't need much more.' Clover remembered that she had been told that she was to have a drink with him after duty. If I'm late, that gives me the perfect let-out, she thought, feeling too raw to have to endure the overtures of another Don Juan. She went to the side ward with supper for the women there. A new patient sat up in bed, looking as if she was enjoying the change of scene and showed no sign of being overawed or frightened at her surroundings. The notes indicated that it was a simple case of fibroids of the uterus, for operation in two days' time, and as yet the patient was able to eat what she liked.

'Mrs Street!' Clover looked again. The patient sat up and smiled, her hair neatly brushed and her eyes brighter. 'You look better.'

'I am better, Nurse, thanks to you and that nice foreign man.'

'Foreign man? Oh, you mean Dr Blamine.' Clover remembered only too vividly why Mrs Street should have the impression that he was foreign, and it wasn't every day a patient heard a surgeon tell a nurse he loved her, even if it was a joke!

'I wondered what he said, afterwards when I calmed down. What was it, Nurse?'

'Oh, he suddenly knew what was wrong and shouted something like eureka! I expect,' she lied.

'Didn't sound like that, but I expect you know best. I was upset.'

'And now?'

'My son came in ever so cross. He said I ought to have told him about my husband long ago. He might have had more sympathy with him, he said. Anyhow, they've got a woman in to look after things and my son looks in every evening to make him take his tablets. He won't come to see me as he hates hospitals, but if I know he's all right I can hurry up and get well.' She leaned over towards Clover. 'They needed that bed for this lady, so poor Mrs Sunderland had to go to the ward. I was sorry to see her go. I expect we shall have to have our operations soon and I was hoping to go up at the same time.'

Clover Dylan opened her mouth to say that Mrs Sunderland had already been to the theatre, but she recalled what Dr Crown had told them about snatching the gland by operating before the patient expected to be sent to the theatre, and so avoiding any panic and sudden rise in heart rate. 'I expect you'll see her soon,' she said. 'But your job is to rest so that your pulse rate settles. Don't think of the operation yet.'

'That nice blond doctor came and talked to me and gave me an injection. He said he would come every day to see me and make sure my heart was all right. Isn't he nice, Nurse?'

'They say that he is charming. I have only met him a couple of times and I'm too junior to bother the big boys,' said Clover lightly.

'I thought you bothered Dr—what's his name, when he was shouting whatever you say he shouted!' Clover blushed. 'Now there's a man for you, Nurse. I think he's very good looking, but you won't have to lead him on, Nurse.'

'As if I would, or could! He has lots of girl-friends and doesn't need me.' Clover finished her jugs and measurements, told the new patient where the sitting-room was and assured her that there was a television there, on all the time, and watched her hurry off to see the latest instalment of the current soap opera. It was one of those peopled with incredibly beautiful beings leading lives beyond the comprehension of simple souls, but bringing a vicarious pleasure to thousands. If life was as simple as that it would be far more bearable, thought Clover.

The last patient from the operating list arrived, and was put to bed with silent efficiency. A nurse sat at the bedside, recording pulse rate and respiration and checking the flow of the intravenous drip. One of the bottles on the stand by the bed of the first patient was nearly empty and Clover told the junior staff nurse.

'Good thing you noticed. I've been so busy that I didn't realise it was time to check. Here, help me change it. You hold the new one. That's fine.' She checked the others and smiled at Clover. 'Tough at first, but you're the kind who will love it.'

Clover warmed to her. It was wonderful to think that she had been really useful and the evening had passed without being told off by anyone. The ward settled, with the dusk growing outside the old hospital and the lights slowly switching on in many departments. High up in the operating theatre that had been in use since early morning, the powerful spot lights dimmed and went out, leaving only the sterilising rooms, the surgeons' room and the office lit brightly. Staff from every ward took it in turns to go down to eat, knowing that there would be appetising food ready for them.

Clover found herself next to Vilma, who seemed subdued. They ate in silence, each one deep in her own thoughts until another nurse joined them and made a casual remark which seemed to awaken them.

'Hard day?' said Clover. Vilma nodded. 'Delia looked even more frantic than usual, I thought when I saw her at the lecture.'

'She's off this evening. I was off this morning and had a letter from Hugo. He has to go away for a while.'

'Is that what's upsetting you?'

'Not exactly. I saw a very ill baby this morning for the first time in my life, and I knew that if I was confronted with that situation when I am married and Hugo and me are working in some remote mission, I could never cope.'

'You've only been here for a week, so how can you know?' Clover tried to smile, but didn't want to be thought flippant. 'They didn't expect you to do anything, did they?'

'No, they didn't, but I had this sudden conviction that I can't do the work. I can work here where everyone is efficient and kind and we have the necessary equipment, but left to make my own decisions, I know it would be a disaster.'

'You can't know that, Vilma. Nobody can tell

what they can do in an emergency until the need arises.' Clover reached over and touched her hand. 'You of all people, Vilma. You were the one at PTS who gave us confidence and you have something that many of us have lost or never had, a faith that will give you strength.'

'Don't you see, girl, that I have lost it too? I saw that child and I was helpless.' The big brown eyes filled with tears. 'There is a staff nurse on that ward who is everything I am against. She is a part-time nurse who happens to be on childrens' for a while. She is lazy and, for the most part, inefficient in the routine work. She came to Beattie's during the last flu epidemic when they were desperately short of staff and seems to have stayed, although she is from an agency, which is against hospital policy. She openly lives with a man and smokes and makes crude jokes on duty when Sister isn't around. God forgive me, but I felt superior to her.' She hung her head.

'And I would think you *should* feel like that,' said Clover, loyally. 'She sounds a heap.'

'She was there when the child came in. The poor little soul was gasping for breath and had an obstruction in her throat. Staff Nurse shouted for someone to bleep the paediatrician and to get a sterilised tracheotomy set. She had the child prepared and the set ready as soon as the doctor came. He took one look and washed his hands. She held the child while he cut and put in the tube. It was all done in five minutes. I shall never forget the rush of air into those tiny lungs and the sigh of relief they both gave as they put on the dressing.'

'What was wrong?'

'She was admitted with a large bead in her throat. On the way up to the ward, she coughed and dislodged it, but it blocked her airway completely. Another minute or two and she might have died.'

'You couldn't know what to do, Vilma. Only a long training could give you the skill and instinct for that kind of decision. By the time you go to your mission, you will be able to cope with anything. You have a great calm, Vilma, and you'd never panic in an emergency.'

'Don't you see? It isn't that, Clover. I was too proud. I thought I was better than that girl and I have failed. At that moment, my faith deserted me and now Hugo is going away and I shall see him only once in the next six months.' She lowered her voice. 'I had been thinking that the girl was immoral, living with a man she couldn't marry, and yet I knew I envied her. I wished that I could be with Hugo, even if we weren't man and wife. I think I hated her for having what I couldn't have.'

'If you love him, of course you want him with you all the time. Any girl in love would have a hard time denying that urge.'

'Would you?'

Clover saw the serious gaze and the bruised innocence of the girl who was her friend. 'I don't know.' She thought of Alex, with his questing hands and wet lips and relived the revulsion she had felt. But there were other hands that were firm and strong and gentle, other eyes that could kindle into humour and something that had made her gasp. If such a man wanted her, could she say no? 'I just can't answer that,' she said, slowly. 'I just don't know what would happen if I was really in love and he loved me.'

'I expect I'm tired.' Vilma sighed. 'I shall have a phone call from Hugo this evening before he leaves for Trinidad and I shall see him briefly in a month's time. Thank you, Clover, you've helped me.'

'I've done nothing. I couldn't even answer a simple question,' Clover said apologetically, feeling perplexed herself.

'Simple? My dear, that's one of the most difficult questions ever asked!' Vilma leant across the table and patted her hand gratefully.

'Come and have some coffee after duty if you feel like it,' Clover offered.

'No, I shall wait for the call which may be late, but I'm all right now. I think that we see so much work that looks difficult and beyond us that our courage fails, sometimes.' She smiled. 'See you later.'

In a way it was comforting to know that someone as organised and as calm as Vilma could feel as she did. I've been sorted out, too, in another way, Clover thought. I suppose I shall live through it all if Dr Blamine keeps out of the picture, but she thought again of what Vilma had asked her, seeing again the honest eyes that would immediately detect a lie.

If Darcy Blamine made love to me, could I resist? It was the first time she had admitted that he had a traumatic effect on her. Now, she let herself remember the kiss that had bruised her lips, and branded her soul as his, if he wanted her, when he wanted her. And he despised her and resented her putting him in an invidious situation.

Sister was ready with a pile of notes to tell her staff of the ward changes and to give them instructions for the next day. She sent Clover to the duty room to fetch her bag as her reading glasses were in it. On the way, Clover saw the lift doors open at the end of the corridor and watched as two men she recognised came towards the ward door.

Hurriedly, she scooped up the bag and hoped that she could get back without meeting them, but a theatre trolley blocked her way as the porter came out of the ward and she had to stop and hold the door aside to let him through. By that time, the two gowned figures had caught up with her.

'Nice work, Clover,' said Dr Richard Crown as if he had known her all her life. She stared at him, trying to look puzzled but succeeding only in looking blank. 'Mrs Street. Her heart has settled well and we may be able to take her up in two days' time, isn't that right, Darcy?'

Dr Blamine still wore the mask he had used for the last case, and the dark blue eyes, the only part of his face that could be seen, gave nothing away. 'That's right,' he said, shortly. 'Is Sister there?'

'She's in the office giving her report, Dr Blamine.' He nodded curtly and strode away.

'That's good news about Mrs Street,' said Clover, trying to sound unconcerned by the surgeon's brusque manner.

'What's got into old Darcy? He's been like a bear with a belly-ache all day. The theatre staff must have wanted him to fall down the nearest manhole. I didn't know he could be so odd. Muttering French curses and throwing swabs as if he wanted to kill someone.'

'Not the patient, I hope?' At least she wasn't the only one to feel the edge of his displeasure.

'No, to watch him do a thyroid is to watch a poem.' Richard kissed the tips of his fingers in ecstasy. 'He's got me going continental, now, but there's no doubt that he is a fine surgeon. In fact, we make a very good team.'

'I have to go. Sister needs her glasses,' said Clover, nervously. She saw Darcy Blamine coming back towards them.

As he came within hearing, Richard Crown said, 'Pick you up about nine. If I'm not there, wait at the lodge. Don't forget.'

'I haven't said I want to come with you.'

'You will . . . they all do,' said the deep voice that made her want to cry. 'Didn't you know it was a part of your training to be made by Richard Crown?' The edge of bitterness deepened. 'I'm sure that an accommodating girl like you will conform to the prevailing customs.'

'One day, I hope you realise how hateful you are, *sir*.' Clover hurried away and hid her red face behind the cloak hanging on the back of the office door, where she could listen to the report and take no part in the discussion.

Most of it was beyond her, even if her mind wasn't in such a turmoil. The new admission, Miss Vicary, was suffering from a disorder of the pituitary gland, a small endocrine gland in a tiny space in a bone at the base of the skull, which secretes several hormones that have a dramatic effect on other endocrine glands. As she listened, Clover couldn't help becoming absorbed in the subject and was full of wonder that such a small gland could have such a wide-spread responsibility for the function of bigger glands.

Miss Vicary had a deficiency of one of the hormones and had been admitted to see if something could be done to make her have regular menstrual periods, first by giving her carefully recorded drugs and then to find if the condition was simple or due to the presence of grossly thickened tissue. X-rays taken that day had given a hopeful result and it was almost certain that there was no tumour present.

'What drugs will she have?' asked one nurse.

'Dr Blamine is prescribing menotrophin to stimulate the follicles in the ovaries, and chorionic gonadotrophin, hoping that this will make the ovaries work normally. If the cycle is restored she will benefit in many ways, and her weight should go down rapidly.' Sister looked round at the fresh young faces, with their bright complexions. 'Poor girl, she isn't old enough to give up hopes of marriage and having children and I think if her appearance improved, she could be a happier person. That moustache, for instance, must be very trying. She said that she used wax for a long time, until she became allergic to it, and then made the fatal mistake of shaving.'

'I've never heard of this particular treatment before, Sister,' said the junior staff nurse.

'It has to be carefully monitored and Dr Blamine brought a very skilled scientist with him to work in the pathology department at the invitation of Dr Pearce, who hopes to continue research into endocrine disorders when Dr Blamine goes back to Canada in a few months' time.'

Clover held her breath. He was going away and she need never hear that voice scarifying her soul, breaking her heart with its contempt. She could continue her training and become a useful member of the staff at the Princess Beatrice Hospital. Three weeks ago, that was her one ambition, and surely it couldn't have changed in such a short time?

'I thought he was here for keeps, Sister. He's a wonderful doctor and a very attractive addition to the furniture,' said another nurse, with a cheeky smile. 'It doesn't give us much time to make use of his talents.'

A buzz of stifled laughter followed her remark and Sister gave her a cool look, although there was a hint of appreciation in that glance. 'Calm down, all of you,' said Sister Scott. 'He's a fine doctor, a good surgeon and a very nice human being when he isn't cross, but I doubt if you have seen the scientist he brought with him. She is very pretty as well as being so efficient that any man would welcome her as a colleague.'

'And he likes efficiency. We'll have to make sure that we are better than she is, girls.' The lecture was over and Clover Dylan hoped that she had taken in even a quarter of the information, but she had scribbled solidly through some of the case histories and knew that she could look at them later. Later? It was late already. She smiled. Nine o'clock, and she had the perfect excuse to back out of the one-sided date that Richard Crown thought was a *fait accompli*. The chattering group scattered at the entrance, to go to their various rooms. Glancing towards the lodge, Clover was relieved to see that Richard Crown was not there. It was only five past nine, but perhaps he had come and gone, only half-believing that she would come with him.

Clover relaxed. There was no further need to be on the defensive. Richard Crown would have no difficulty in finding another companion for the evening. Alex had gone too, and the rest of the night could be spent in nun-like seclusion in her room, cosily tucked up with dressing-gown and hot cocoa. I could even wash my hair, she thought, remembering the half-serious remarks of the handsome anaesthetist. She turned to the brightly-lit entrance of the home. It seemed very pointed to make no effort to be friendly with Richard Crown. No strings with him unless she made the running, she began to believe. She thought of the dark blue eyes that shone with scathing fire and her pride refused to be put down. I've done nothing wrong apart from forgetting that one man was a diabetic, and that shouldn't have been the responsibility of a nurse on her first day, she told herself reasonably. I am rapidly developing a guilt complex over things that he has no right to condemn, and what I do with my spare time is my own affair, she told herself. A beautiful scientist? He had no need of other feminine company then. Was that the reason why he was so remote?

Clover went to her room and stripped off her uniform. She stood in her bikini pants and bra and slid her fingers over her slim waist and thighs. Other men would find her desirable and why should she carry a torch for a man who treated her so badly? It might be sensible to do so if she had the remotest hope that he would notice her as a woman to be loved, but surely, her vanity couldn't tell her that it could ever happen. She pulled a silk shirt on and tucked it into the waistband of bright emerald green pants. The vivid colour of the violet shirt made her look like an exotic tropical flower.

She added a rope of dull red beads that hung carelessly over and under the open neck of the shirt in four rows, and her flat bronze sandals added to the bohemian picture. She brushed her hair and saw the auburn lights appear. With an expression of repugnance, she threw the lipstick she had used the night that Alex had tried to rape her into the waste bin and selected a soft pinky tone that blended with the other colours and gave her a slightly ethereal pallor.

Hell, if Richard asked any of the others if I got

ready for a date with him, at least they can tell him
that I did, she assured her reflection, even though I
was too late off duty to keep the appointment.
Clover decided to go downstairs to make coffee,
then thought she might listen to music in the small
room reserved for that purpose. As she came
downstairs she saw Vilma, curled up on a big chair
near the door in the sitting room, waiting for the
phone call from Hugo with all the patience and
resignation of a dutiful fiancée.

I could wait around for someone for ever and
waste half of my life yearning for something out of
my reach, thought Clover. I must forget him and try
to think that he never came here. In a few months it
will be as if he had never left Canada and I can have
a normal training. It's all right for Vilma, she
reflected. Hugo loves her and she is safe in that
love, even if they have to wait. Her eyes were
dreamy, as unbidden memories came back of the
man who had taken her heart and nearly all her
pride. If he loved me, would I wait for him? What a
question . . . The pressure on her lips and the
hardness of his embrace had told her that waiting
wouldn't be possible if he returned her love. She
shuddered as a finger of ice touched her spine.
There was desire sleeping in the depths of the
dark blue pools of his eyes, gentleness and in-
stinctive knowledge in the hands that could
school a woman's body, and passion that would
flare into a hot white flame if he met the woman of
his life.

'He's not for me, so I must take what I can from

life. There was little consolation in that, though. I will give myself to my work, but apart from that, I'll find amusement with such people as Richard Crown, she decided—and was hardly surprised to find him in the kitchen, sipping coffee with Rosalyn. He smiled, delightedly.

'For me?' he said.

'I couldn't come in uniform,' she said, flatly. 'I always dress like this when I go to the WVS.'

'Robin telephoned,' said Rosalyn. 'I told him you were still on duty so we had a little chat. You didn't appear and I said that you had a date this evening, so he said to tell you hello and he'll meet you soon.'

'You seem to know a lot about my comings and goings,' said Clover. 'Nice to be told what I'm to do. I didn't think I would be going out. You said nine, and I was still on duty then,' she said to Richard with a slight smile.

'But you were worth waiting for.' He put the mug back on the draining board and picked up the velvet jacket he had slung over the arm of the wooden chair.

'Are you coming, Ros?' It was her last gesture to having a chaperon with Richard Crown.

'I'm not a gooseberry,' said Rosalyn, in a whispered aside. 'But don't get too involved. We have a date with Robin and a friend the day after tomorrow.'

'Great,' said Clover, mildly. 'I won't elope tonight in that case.' She turned to Richard. 'Well, if you want to buy me that drink, shall we go? I have to be back soon to read up a load of notes about the ward.'

'No need,' he said, smoothly. 'Just ask me anything and I'll put you in the picture.'

'I prefer to read the notes that Sister gave me. You would tell me everything from the medical point of view, but I have to learn the mundane details at my stage in training. I have to know the details of fluid intake and output charts, diets and treatment and who doesn't have a pitcher of water on her locker.'

'All high-powered stuff,' he said, gravely. 'But honestly, Clover, if you didn't learn all that boring stuff, the ward wouldn't be able to run. Good nursing can be felt as soon as the ward door opens. Sister Scott runs a very crisp ship.'

'She's pretty, too.' Clover looked sideways.

'Very,' he said, 'but she has wedding rings in her eyes.'

'Would that be bad?' Clover began to enjoy herself as they walked across the park under the sighing trees, past the Victorian monument with the broken nose, and the empty paddling pool that couldn't be used because the local vandals used it as a dump for beer bottles and old cans. She hadn't ventured into the park alone, wondering if it was safe to do so, but on a fine summer evening it held no threat and she was surprised to find how countrified it was, away from the road. Late birds scolded on their way to roost and a group of teenagers were trying to make music on an old guitar, a comb and paper and an oil drum. Richard threw some coins down and the boys laughed, saying that they'd send him tickets when they hit the Albert Hall.

The noise followed them as they wandered along the winding path that led to the top entrance near the Falcon, the busy restaurant with its bars that attracted so many of the staff at Beattie's. She smiled. Richard was fun and an unwilling affection for him stirred within her. If he could be a friend to her at Beattie's, it could be good. What stupid ideas I had while I was changing this evening, she decided. I couldn't have an affair with Richard. She liked him far too much to waste her feelings for him on a brief love affair that would leave them distant—perhaps even enemies.

He put a friendly hand on her arm to point her in the direction of a corner table that was still unoccupied and from where they could watch the rest of the chattering clients of the Falcon. Clover said she'd like some cider and shook her head when Richard asked if she was hungry. He came back from the bar with beer and cider, a plate of biscuits and cheese and some potato crisps.

'I didn't have dinner,' he said. She was mildly curious. 'You see, a child had a bleeding tonsil and I couldn't leave until I was quite sure she was all right. I always wait for at least half an hour after a secondary bleeding. By that time, it's cleared up or back in the theatre.'

'But you were in the main theatre, weren't you?'

He shrugged. 'I stood in for the guy who did Ts and As and said I'd be on call until nine. It was just my luck to get the bleed. However, I actually like bread and cheese and beer! Or would you rather have it, *A flask of wine, a loaf of bread and thou?*' he misquoted.

She laughed. 'I'd rather sit here than under a tree, thank you, however idyllic it sounds, and cider will do nicely!'

The room was filling fast and Clover recognised several people from the hospital including Sister Scott, who seemed surprised to see her. Richard eyed her with pleasure but there was no imminent heavy breathing and they found that they had a lot in common. Indulgently, he pointed out the more colourful characters and had her laughing at some of the obviously highly libellous stories he told about them. He looked round to find more victims to be verbally dissected by his caustic wit and smiled at a couple pausing in the doorway, who seemed undecided whether to come into the lounge or to go to the restaurant. Darcy Blamine put up a casual hand and urged his companion towards the couple sitting at the small table.

'Room for us?' he asked.

'Sure. Hello, Chantal, have they let you out of your test-tubes?' Richard joked, but he was unable to take his eyes from the vision in front of them.

Clover stared too. Chantal's muted suede skirt was linked to the black shirt by a many-thonged leather belt that bore the logo of a very famous fashion house. The enormous coral necklace hung warmly on the deeply tanned throat, so that there was more coral than shirt covering her firm high bosom, and her hair was fashionably wild with the studied and careful coiffeuring necessary to obtain that effect without making the hair like a bird's nest. Long fine hands moved restlessly to settle the cashmere jacket over the back of her seat and then she turned to Richard with a bright smile.

''Allo, Richard.' The voice was husky and caressing, the eyes deep and calculating.

'You haven't met?' Clover shook her head, dumbly. 'Chantal, this is Clover, one of our new members of staff. She is going to run Beattie's one day unless someone kidnaps her and takes her away.'

'Keednap? Ah, yes, she is a child. 'Allo,' said Chantal. With those words Chantal seemed to dismiss Clover as a necessary evil to be tolerated if she was to have drinks with two handsome men.

'Hello,' said Clover weakly. Suddenly, the colours of her striking outfit were garish and harsh, her make-up was all wrong and she knew she ought to have stayed in to wash her hair, or better still, to bury her head in a textbook and turn her attention to the only thing left to her, a career in nursing. No way was it possible that Darcy Blamine could look at another woman when Chantal was near. He had brought her with him, and Clover supposed that when he went back to Canada, she would go too. They shared an interest of great importance and it was the kind of interest that could be combined with marriage, living together or a casual affair. Looking at Chantal, it seemed impossible that one of those arrangements was not already in being.

CHAPTER SEVEN

It was raining as Nurse Clover Dylan walked over to the main part of the hospital. The small umbrella did nothing to protect her legs and the hem of her skirt and she wished she had worn her cloak even though it was hot and thundery with more heat to come. The leaves on the plane trees hung limply or were thrown up, showing their undersides as the wet wind took them. The weather matched her mood and she dreaded going on the ward and having to be bright and good-humoured when she did the morning blanket baths.

A quick glance at the report book, left open by the night staff so that nurses coming on for the morning shift could see at a glance what had happened during the night, showed that there had been an emergency. Mrs Wendy Roper had been admitted at midnight with acute abdominal pain and sent to the ward for admission and diagnosis as there was no really experienced doctor on duty in casualty and her condition showed that she had a degree of shock.

'What happened?' Clover asked a night nurse who was tidying the sluice room and putting out the washing trays, ready for the next shift to use.

'A bit of a flap, but it made a change. She came in with no notice. She'd been out for the evening and collapsed in the Tube on the way home. When she came in, she was shocked and was suffering from biliary colic. She had eaten a heavy meal and was being sick, which was a good thing as it cleared her stomach before she had an anaesthetic. We passed a stomach tube and aspirated the rest and it relieved her a little, but she was still having bouts of severe pain. The tiny stones from her gall bladder were escaping into the alimentary tract.'

'How did they know it was her gall bladder? She couldn't have been able to say much if she collapsed.' Clover wanted to know more.

Her husband was there. He said she had several attacks when they lived in the north and the doctors said that if it happened again, they'd have to operate. She is slightly jaundiced and feeling very sorry for herself, with tubes sticking out in every direction.'

Clover hurried off to complete her bed baths and washings, helped with bed pans and tidied before the breakfast trolley came up to the ward. She was anxious to see the new patient, but she was behind curtains in the bed close to Sister's office door, where she could be observed easily. When she did get a chance to look, Clover wished she hadn't bothered to do so. She saw a woman with a yellowish face lying propped up on two pillows with an intravenous tube in one arm, a tube down through one nostril to her stomach, so that fluid and wind could be withdrawn by syringe and so lessen the tension in her stomach and discourage vomiting, and a tube came from under the bedclothes down into a bottle fixed to the side of the bed.

How could anyone survive after looking like that? How would a nurse begin to care for such a case?

'Don't just stand there. If you've finished your work and are waiting to give out breakfast to the bed patients, you have time to help me with this lady.' Sister Scott came from her office, having read the report. The new nurse blenched visibly. 'Come on, Nurse. Don't look so scared. You'll have to deal with worse than this before you finish training. That is, *if* you finish training.'

It was going to be bad, Clover knew. Since Sister Scott saw her with Richard Crown last night in the Falcon, Clover had a feeling that she was no longer in Sister's good books. Sister seemed quite pleased to see the young nurse's reluctance to help with the post-operative case who looked so ill. Clover bit her lip and moved near the bed. Even the whites of the patient's eyes were yellow and the woman looked listless, deep in her state of half-deadened pain and weakness.

'Come closer, Nurse.' Sister's voice was gentle, now. This was not a personal matter. Here, they were just two nurses caring for a sick person and that was their chief priority. This was no time for displeasure or friction, and Clover lost her fear as she helped to lift the woman, smooth her sheets and make her comfortable on one more pillow, taking care that none of the tubes were disturbed during the movement.

'We want to get her into Fowler's position as

soon as possible to drain the mucus and bile from the tube. From the X-rays, it shows that the stones were fragmented, and not every particle has been taken away. Dr Blamine said in the notes that there were some bits stuck in the common bile duct, so the drain must stay in until we have another X-ray tomorrow or the next day to see that it is clear. That's why she had so much pain. If the stone had been very large, it couldn't have come down the tube and blocked it. But once a small piece comes away and leaves room for more to work down, there is a continuous risk of biliary colic, or severe pain as the stone passes along the thin tube to the bowel. If it is inflamed, you can be sure that the pain is excruciating.'

'Will she be all right, Sister?' whispered Clover.

'Of course. She had the very best attention. Dr Blamine may be specialising in endocrinology but he is a first class general surgeon. That's how he came here, on a year's exchange with one of Beattie's men.'

'But Dr Blamine was in the Falcon last night.'

'Weren't we all?' Now they were away from the patient, her tone was bleak. 'I hope you enjoyed your evening.'

'Yes, thank you, Sister. I didn't stay for long as I had notes to write up and learn for today, but I enjoyed the break.' Clover tried to play it all down.

But Sister Scott looked as if she didn't want to believe her. She had come in with two other Sisters, had one drink and departed, with only the coolest wave to Darcy Blamine and no recognition of Richard or the rest of the party. How was she to know that when the rain began to pour down a mere half-hour after she left, Darcy had taken them all back to the hospital in his car?

It had been tipping down by then and everyone had run for cover when the car drew up at the hotel. At the time, Clover thought that Darcy had asked Richard to hold the umbrella over Chantal because he wanted her, at least, to be protected. But there was also a sneaking suspicion that Dr Blamine had no intention of allowing Clover to end the evening in the company of the blond anaesthetist! Chantal had clutched Richard's arm and snuggled close under the umbrella, while Clover paddled her way through to the hostel. The others went into the main block, from where they could reach the medical quarters in the dry

Clover had heard that Chantal was staying here, in the big, old-fashioned rooms overlooking the tennis courts that had belonged to the old part of the hospital, and which, from the outside, still looked severe and institutional. Darcy Blamine didn't live there, but shared a flat with an old colleague not far from the hospital. Glancing back at the three figures so close together, Clover felt excluded and wondered if he would bother to go back to the flat that night. It would be so easy to stay in the medical quarters, especially if he was invited to do so by the lovely and, Clover suspected, predatory Chantal.

'I suppose you couldn't have been there all that long,' conceded Sister Scott, grudgingly. 'From the report, I see that Mrs Roper was admitted at eleven o'clock last night and Dr Blamine was making a late round to check on the thyroidectomies done yesterday. He saw her and told the night staff to give her a relaxant which might release the stones, but if her condition got worse to call him and he would operate.'

'It was lucky that Dr Crown came back with him, Sister,' said Clover, demurely. 'I suppose Dr Blamine stayed in the hospital with Dr Crown, on call?' she suggested.

'No.' Sister smiled, suddenly confident that the new and very pretty nurse had not been with Dr Crown late at night, alone. 'As a matter of fact, Dr Blamine went over to the room reserved for surgeons on call. It's kept for those who need to stay near the hospital but are usually non-resident.'

Clover felt her mouth go dry. He had been sleeping under the same roof, in the same corridor as her room! She had seen the small notice on the door, saying that it was reserved for visiting surgeons, and when Alex came to her demanding that he allow him to stay, she had wondered if she could have permission to use it. But she'd soon realised it was impossible. Such rooms needed to be ready for occupation at a moment's notice, and she smiled as she imagined what would be said when a tired man arrived from the operating theatre at four in the morning to find a student snoring away in his bed.

'He must be tired, Sister. Both of them must be tired.'

'Yes. I wonder if they are awake?' A slow smile spread over Sister's face. 'Breakfasts all finished? Good.' She seemed to come to a decision. 'I think I'll take my coffee away from the ward, Nurse. I want to be back early for Sir Horace, who is coming to see the lady with fibroids. She was once an employee of his and he promised that if she needed to come in, he would visit her, and if necessary come back to Beattie's from retirement to do the operation.'

'Yes, Sister.' Clover couldn't think why she should be the one to receive all this explanation.

'I see that we are well on in the ward. Take your coffee break now and when you are in the home, take some coffee and toast to Dr Blamine. I'll write a note about Mrs Roper so that he has no need to rush over.' She looked faintly embarrassed. 'I'll do the same for Dr Crown. I think it best if a sister goes into the medical school. It isn't a place where nurses are allowed except on business. I can put him in the picture.' She looked as if she needed to justify her visit. 'He is a very good doctor and cares deeply about his patients,' she said.

'I had that impression, too, Sister.' There was nothing in her eyes to make Sister Scott think that Clover was interested in Dr Crown, and the senior nurse looked pleased.

'Use the things from the kitchen in the hostel and take some bread from the ward in case the supply over there hasn't been delivered. There is marmalade in the top cupboard for general use and if he wants honey, take some from my locker. It's open and I think there's enough there.'

As Clover went past the kitchen door, after washing her hands and collecting her cloak, she saw Sister preparing a veritable feast for the lucky anaesthetist. No toast and honey for him! Scrambled eggs and bacon, sister's own good china and the very best black cherry preserve were being prepared for him. Clover thought it was all very amusing.

It was with a strange feeling of shyness that she approached the hostel. How was she to stand by the bed of the man she loved and make mundane statements about the weather and did he sleep well? She knew she would want to touch him, to wonder if at last he might smile at her, to fantasise about the impossible time when he would look on her with love in those dark blue eyes . . .

She made strong coffee and put it in a tall brown jug that she found and washed. She took the top of two bottles of creamy milk that she found in the fridge and left them looking rather diluted. The cream she put into the old dark green jug that she had brought from home. Her grandmother had given it to her when she was taking exams at school and she had kept it close to her ever since.

I was scared of exams even then, she recalled, holding the jug, and she knew that her feelings had changed very little. I'm scared of life, even though I'm officially a woman, grown and educated, with enough intelligence to take me through most situations with ease, she thought. Despite her fears the tray was ready and she had no choice but to go up to his room if he was to have hot coffee. It's my coffee time, too, she thought and took another cup to her room, ready to drink it in there once she had left the tray. Then she went down the corridor and tapped at his door. There was no reply. She glanced down at the tray and saw the words on the Cornish pottery jug. She turned it so that they weren't obvious. Perhaps he won't notice, she thought. How corny they were, that old rhyme that had given her real courage when she had first received the jug.

Ah, well! They still fit me. I shall never reach my heart's desire, she thought ruefully, and as she pushed open the door, calling softly, the words came back to her:

> Do what you can
> Being what you are
> Shine like a glow worm
> If you can't be a star.

'Dr Blamine,' she said, quietly as she put the tray on the table. His clothes were strewn untidily over the chair and his socks were on the floor. One shoe lay half under the bed and the other, for a reason that wasn't clear, was on the dressing table as if it had been thrown there after he was in bed. He was deeply asleep and she looked at the tray and then at him. She couldn't stay until he woke up in his own time and by then, the coffee would be cold. I have to go back on duty, she thought, but had a feeling that she might be back before Sister Scott, on her errand of mercy.

He stirred and she backed away as the bare arm came from under the bedclothes, but he was only turning over in his sleep, murmuring words in French that she couldn't catch.

'Dr Blamine,' she said. The other arm came into sight, and she saw his bare chest as he lay on his back, his head to one side. The tendons in the neck were like bronze cords and Clover wondered where he had been to get so much sun. Chantal had a good tan, too. The dark hairs curled on the brown skin, making a disappearing arrow of softness below the line of the white sheet. Clover clasped her hands in front of her to keep them from touching his chin, where the arrogant cleft now seemed only beautiful and had no hard edges. The weariness of the night lay on his eyes and he murmured, without indicating that he knew there was anyone in the room.

A glint from under the thick eyelashes focused on her as she stood against the light from the doorway, her hair haloing her head under the tiny white cap. He pushed down the bedclothes still further and she widened her eyes, suddenly scared. He had only a few inches to spare before she would see him completely naked on the bed. As it was, she saw a likeness to one of the ancient gods, sculpted with only a drape of fabric over his loins. His beauty was undeniable and the vision of him lying asleep etched itself deep into her mind and heart. She caught her breath sharply and he opened his eyes.

Sleepily, he put out a hand and she had no alternative but to put hers in it.

He drew her closer and she went, as if sharing his dream. 'The hills are wind blown,' he said. 'And you keep close to the ground, trembling.'

He *must* be dreaming.

The slow smile widened. 'Clover, that little flower that grows wild.'

She tried to pull away but he held her. He had been awake! He must have been awake all the time she stood there looking like a moonstruck calf. It was too bad. He was mocking her again.

'I brought some coffee,' she said, still backing away.

He sat up, pulled by the effort she made to escape and his arms were round her, enveloping her in masculine strength and the hardness of a body made for action and love. The kiss that seemed to take away her will and resistance came sweetly to her mouth and she could smell a curious mixture of masculine sweat, ether and cologne. She shut her eyes and wondered if death was as all enveloping, as final as her commitment in that one embrace. His grip became tighter and sanity began to surface again. She pushed him away, turning her head so that the kisses he sought to take and to give could not find her lips. She knew that if she didn't escape, her body would betray her into a passion that couldn't be controlled, and she knew that there was no love in his heart.

'No,' she said, and fell off the bed, dragging the blanket with her. She sat on the floor, her cap hanging by one pin and her dress undone to the waist. 'You mustn't,' she said, weakly. 'I only brought the coffee!'

The urgency of desire left his eyes and the dark blue was once more still waters that glinted with malice. He held the sheet lightly as if it was of no consequence whether it fell to the floor and left him completely naked or remained to cover him.

'You brought me some breakfast. Are you not to share it with me?'

She shook her head, struggling to her feet, conscious that her tights were laddered and she must get to her room at once before anything more happened. She backed away to the door, glanced out at the blessedly empty corridor, and fled, her pride shattered completely by his last cynical remark.

'I thought it was all a part of the service,' he called after her.

Clover gulped her cup of coffee in the safety of her own room and changed her tights. She brushed her hair and put on a fresh cap. To see her, no one would dream that anything untoward had happened in the darkened room at the end of the corridor, but she was in a state of emotional shock. Her new awareness of the force of desire was frightening. She had some idea now of the danger, and the inevitability of her desire reaching a point of no return and she trembled. But if she loved Darcy Blamine, she would feel nothing for other men. That would be her safeguard during the time of her training. People like Richard could come and go and wonder why the girl with the passionate mouth would not sleep with them, and she would be safe in her own frustration and loneliness.

She took her cup down to the kitchen and drank more coffee, needing the hot bitter taste and the reviving scent that blotted out the scent of a man's body, close to hers. She picked up her cloak and the note from Sister Scott fell out of the pocket. I can't go back to his room, she thought, panic-stricken, but I must send it to him. A tiny smile, tremulously made its appearance as her sense of proportion reasserted itself. A sound from a room two doors away told her that other nurses were coming for the coffee break.

'Delia,' she called. 'Would you mind taking this to Dr Blamine in the visitor's room? I have to fly. Sister wants me back early.' Delia looked pleased. 'Just tap on the door and go in,' said Clover.

Delia hurried along and tapped on the door. A voice said, 'Come in,' and as Clover hurried by to the stairs, she heard an annoyed *Merde!*'

Sister Scott was not in the ward and the staff nurse was busy coping with Sir Hector, who was in full sail, talking to any patient he passed in his royal progress along the row of cubicles. He even asked about the patients who were still behind drawn curtains. In vain, Staff Nurse tried to steer him out to see his one patient. But old habits die hard, and he had ruled the department for so long, in charge of all the gynaecology beds there, that he was delighted to be back in an official capacity and wanted to make the visit last.

At last he demanded coffee and went into the side ward to see his patient while it was being prepared. Staff Nurse whispered to the junior nurse to tell her when the coffee was ready. 'I'll never get down to dressings if he stays,' she said. 'I can't think where Sister can be.'

Clover said nothing but couldn't help wondering if taking a man his breakfast in bed wasn't the signal for a fate worse than death—although the thought of Sister Scott being dragged into bed against her will was mind-boggling! As she filled the silver coffee pot that Sister reserved for her own use and for the few favoured visitors asked to share it, Clover remembered the green jug with the silly rhyme on the side. Apart from any disquiet she might feel that he would read it and laugh, the jug did belong to her and she treasured it as a kind of comfortable talisman, echoing the security of her infant days. I'll slip over at lunch time and find it, she thought, and then the work of the ward closed round her, making any other worries impossible. Soon Sister arrived back, looking pink-cheeked and in a very good mood, and without even a smear of marmalade or cherry jam to show any activity!

It was better to take a cynical view—to take it for granted that all hospital doctors were so self-opinionated that they thought all the nurses were a fair target for their intentions, however much they were repulsed. I must think of Dr Blamine as a lecher, or I shall never manage to meet him again and act as if nothing happened, Clover schooled herself. The men she had repulsed in the past had taken the hint and some had actually become good friends, but she had never been emotionally aware of *them*.

This was different. Could she control her own reaction to his nearness if she had to work with him at a bedside? Clover doubted it. But she was not put to the test, for neither Dr Blamine or Dr Crown made an appearance that morning. After lunch, she returned to the ward and went to the office. There were two figures inside, and one was a man. She hesitated, then tapped on the frosted glass, knowing that she *had* to report off duty—she couldn't just leave without telling Sister.

Richard Crown grinned when she entered the room. 'Another woman who slept the night away while poor old Darcy and I coped with a horrendous gall bladder!'

Clover gave him an unfriendly look. He was laughing as if he might have been sharing a joke with Sister before they saw her and they still found her funny.

'I'm sorry you lost your beauty sleep,' she said. 'May I report off duty, Sister?'

'Yes, Nurse, you may go.' As Clover turned away, she called her back. 'You have this afternoon and tomorrow? What are you due? Ah, yes.' She held the off-duty rota in her hand. 'An evening and then your day off. I'm sorry, Nurse, but I think you'll have to take your day off on Sunday. You can have an evening tomorrow, but I'm afraid you have to take some more patients to the exams in the morning. That usually lasts all day, taking into account the time spent fetching and sending them home again. As you did it without losing a patient, Admin thought they might as well send you again. You don't mind, do you?'

'No, Sister.' It would be a relief to be away from the hospital for a day now that she knew Dr Blamine would be busy in the ward or working with Chantal on his pet project. Or projects, she thought, bleakly, remembering the casual and elegant sensuality of the French woman.

'Right. Come back this evening, and tomorrow report to the minibus as you did the last time. If you want to stay in town to shop or meet friends, do so. You can take a dress and change at Bart's if you wish, once you have seen the last of your flock away safely. If this weather lasts, you could do worse than explore St Katharine's Dock. It's quite a place.' Sister looked dreamy and Richard Crown smiled in such a way that Clover knew that they had been there, together.

'I might do that,' she said. 'I'll take a map of London with me.'

'Be careful. Don't get picked up by a dangerous character,' said Richard, half seriously, as he looked at the good legs and slim waist of the auburn-haired nurse.

'If I can handle the men I've met here, I think I can cope with anyone,' she said and left, closing the door carefully behind her. In spite of her brave words, it could be lonely and embarrassing to go to such a place on her own. She had heard of the development near Tower Bridge where beautiful old ships with many types of sail were anchored in a yacht basin surrounded by cobbled walk ways and interesting buildings. Would she ever manage to go there? Alex would have taken her, and if she had kept the attention of Richard Crown, he would have taken full advantage of such a setting to soften her resistance. It might even be the place where he took all his girl-friends, judging by the soft expression in Sister Scott's eyes when she referred to it.

As she passed the telephone in the hostel it rang, making her start. Her first reaction was to ignore it, thinking it couldn't be for her. Then she felt guilty because on other occasions someone had bothered to hurry up to the stairs to tell her there was a call for her, and surely she ought to pay back the favour.

'Nurses' hostel, The Princess Beatrice,' she said.

'Ah, I wonder if you could take a message?' The voice was husky and sharply accented. 'I think that Dr Blamine is there. He is staying there for a night or so. I am Dr Chantal Delonde. I want him to pick me up at the Cumberland Hotel in an hour.'

'I don't know if he is still here,' began Clover. 'He may be in the theatre or doing a ward round. Can you wait while I look upstairs in his room?'

'I cannot wait. If he is not there, find him.' The line was dead but seemed to hum with the peremptory voice long after the receiver was back on the rest.

'Of all the nerve!' said Clover.

'Someone annoying you even more than I do?'

'Oh, Dr Blamine, I was coming to find you.'

'You were?' He sat on the bench by the door and stretched his long body into a shaft of sunlight. 'How good to hear it. Does that mean that you have forgiven me for upsetting you this morning?' His eyes were languorous and yet there was a sharp glint of curiosity there. 'What did I do this morning? I forget. I was dreaming that a girl with flowers in her hair, like the little flowers on the downs, all soft and purple with green leaves that are trefoil in shape, came and kissed me while I slept.'

Clover blushed scarlet. 'You're teasing me, and it isn't fair.'

'I didn't dream it? You came and kissed me? *C'etait vrai?*' He leaned forward, his eyes serious. 'I have the memory of a kiss and I think you still remember.'

'It wasn't like that and I should think you would want to forget your behaviour, not mock me with something I want to forget.' There were tears in her eyes. He was wonderful, magically attractive and terribly cruel. Did all men with that power treat their women so? But I'm not his woman, she told herself, bringing her mind away from strong arms and the rapture of his kiss. 'That was a message for you from Dr Delonde. You are to meet her in an hour at the Cumberland.'

'Must I?' His eyebrows were raised, the mouth took on a disdainful twist. 'I *must*?' He frowned. 'I cannot think that Chantal used those words!'

'Her exact words were that she wanted you to pick her up at the Cumberland Hotel in an hour, and if you weren't in your room, I was to find you. She then put down the phone as if that was sufficient to send the whole hospital searching for you. Obviously, she knew that you would do exactly what she wanted.' It was bitchy, but not to be resisted.

'And you would have done what she told you to do?'

'I was on my way to you with a note which I would have written in my room. If you had not been there, I would have slipped the note under your door and gone to my own off duty.' Clover tried to make it sound as if she wasn't purposely avoiding him.

'And let me miss my conference?' His gaze was steady and serious. 'I am due at a conference at four and I have to pick up Dr Delonde and take her there. She is an important part of the team.'

'Oh, I thought that . . .' she faltered.

'You thought that she was being thoroughly female, as indeed she is. Do you think she is elegant? Beautiful? Soignée?' The words were like darts into Clover's wounded heart.

'Yes,' she said. 'She is very beautiful.'

'Then I must not keep her waiting, must I?' He took Clover's hand and kissed it. 'Many thanks for delivering the message. It was one I wanted to hear.'

She dragged her hand away and he shook his head. 'It is so strange. The British can never take a graceful compliment. You have pretty fingertips, Clover.'

'Please go,' she said, stiffly. 'I can think of nothing you do or say to me as a compliment. You are a very cruel man.'

The last was whispered and came to him as a sigh on the wind as she rushed past him and up the stairs to her room. He gazed after her thoughtfully for a full minute, a half smile on his lips.

CHAPTER EIGHT

'WHAT's made you so bright?' Rosalyn looked with amazement at the laughing face of Vilma who sat down by her side at breakfast and hugged her.

'You had your phone call,' guessed Clover.

'I want to hug the whole world,' said Vilma, looking as if she must be high on some very sophisticated drug whose only effect was to generate pure joy. And pure joy was in her full dark eyes. It was infectious and even Clover, who had slept badly and felt very depressed, couldn't stop the rush of warmth she felt for the nurse who had been so sad only a day or so ago.

'Hugo and I are going to marry before he goes to Trinidad. I saw Matron yesterday and she gave us her blessing. She said that I would work better while he's away if I am settled in my mind. That woman is a genius to know how I feel.'

'What happened?' said Delia, who had come in late and missed a few sentences.

'We get married next month and have four days together before he goes away.'

'Is that wise? Do you think you can bear to leave him once you are married?'

'It's the uncertainty that is so unsettling. We agreed that this was best for both of us. A married man is looked on as more acceptable in some places and I want to know that once we can be together, we can just be together all the time.' She began to eat with evident enjoyment. 'And it has its practical side,' she said, as if to tone down the joyful self-indulgence. 'Once we are married, Hugo can go ahead and book tickets for us and make the arrangements necessary for a married couple and not for two single people.'

'What a very sensible attitude,' said Rosalyn, with a mocking smile. 'I must remember that when I go away, it is much cheaper to sleep with someone than to have separate rooms. I know one person who would go along with that.' She looked at Clover, and wondered if she was still upset over Alex.

'Don't tease her,' said Clover. 'It's indecent to mention Alex in the same breath as these beautiful souls. I'm green with envy. If I loved someone, I'd want to do as you are doing. You'll leave behind a lot of frustrated women who must try to sublimate their feelings in their work.' It was said lightly, but Rosalyn saw a glimpse of pain in the green eyes.

'You don't think we are rushing into something?' Vilma didn't need their opinions, but she did want their support.

'I think you are very brave and very wise,' said Clover softly.

'I can settle down to work, now,' said Vilma.

'Why are you carrying that bag on duty?' Delia looked at Clover's soft flight bag, curiously. 'I thought you were on this morning. You're in uniform so it can't be your day off.'

'I have to go to Bart's again. They have another batch of students today and I am needed to take a few patients along.'

'Why you each time?' Delia began to think she might be missing something.

'Would you like to go? The last time I went, I was told off for chatting to patients and that lovely man you all find so charming, Dr Blamine, made me have lunch in the hospital in case I talked to students.' She didn't know why she spoke of him, but to mention his name in a way that showed that she disliked him, and that he was very unreasonable, was a relief and might in time convince her that he was as bad as she had once thought him to be.

'Dr Blamine? You're welcome to him,' said Delia with surprising vehemence. 'You know I took that message along to him? He was very rude. First of all he was standing there wearing only a pair of underpants.' She grinned. 'That was all right. Quite a thrill, actually, but then he looked so angry when he saw me that I just left the note and fled. I wouldn't have thought he was as modest as all that, would you? He *did* say come in, and then seemed quite put out when he saw me. I suppose he thought it might be a man with the message.' She preened herself. 'To see a girl when you're in that state of undress must be shattering if you aren't used to it.'

'Quite shattering for a man like Dr Blamine,' said Clover, in a faint voice that hid her laughter. 'Such a modest man,' she added. He must have been certain that it was going to be her who walked through the door! Clover felt a hint of triumph that she had managed to embarrass him, even a little. It raised her spirits. Today, she could go away knowing that he was far too busy to go to the examinations, as Richard had told her of their schedule for the rest of the week. Some of the time Darcy Blamine would be at other centres of medical research, probably with the lovely Chantal, and he was demonstrating an operation on the cortex of the pituitary gland in another hospital.

The sun was coming out and the air was clear once more after a few final sharp claps of thunder. The minibus stood in the wet car park at an angle to allow people to step on board without splashing through the many puddles left after the rain. There were four patients this time and none of them was a thyroid case. The diabetic man was there and the acromegaly, who seemed to be enjoying his brief fame as a fairly unusual case. Another man had a mild heart condition that gave him no trouble and wasn't likely to be dangerous, but would give the students something to think about when they listened in to his chest. The last patient was a woman who walked with care and had perpetually shaking hands. The notes showed that she had Parkinson's disease and was responding well to treatment, but had sufficient symptoms left to make diagnosis fairly easy.

But as Clover knew, the diagnosis wasn't the end of the test. The examining doctor would then want to know the possible treatment, the short term effects of drugs and the long term prognosis for the patient. Listening to the questions and answers had been absorbing, and she knew that once she met the conditions on the wards, she would have no difficulty in recognising them again and knowing what would be done.

They piled into the bus and once more the passenger seat by the driver was empty. Clover put her case under the seat and talked to the patients, trying to water down the lurid accounts that the man with acromegaly was telling. The drive-way to the hospital was busy when they arrived. There was a minibus from another hospital and the nurse with that batch looked at Clover's badge and smiled.

'My sister trained at Beattie's,' she said. 'Lucky you. I lost my place as I had a broken arm just when PTS started. I couldn't be fitted in for ages after that so I had to go elsewhere.'

They chatted until the call came to take the patients to the cubicles for examination. There was a new bundle of magazines and the heart case was soon absorbed in back numbers of a yachting magazine, although, as he confessed, he never went sailing as he was always seasick.

The morning passed quickly and everyone seemed to be in a good humour. Students no longer seemed stunned by the status of the men and women who asked the questions and most of them scored well in their diagnoses. Once or twice it was difficult not to help when Clover knew the answer that surely must be obvious to even the least of medical minds.

I knew nothing only a few weeks ago before I

went to PTS. Now, I am bursting with answers as if I knew more than I have been taught! The thought amused her. The heart murmur was listened to and the poor man got quite used to having stone cold stethoscopes planted on his chest by nervous fingers. Each time, the student was told that the first requisite for any examination was warm hands and a warm stethoscope! The nurse had every sympathy for the students. Who could have warm hands if they were under stress? They'd either be cold or so hot and moist with fear as to be equally unpleasant to touch, she decided.

The sun shone brightly now as if to say sorry for the thunderstorm. It would be lovely to sit out under some trees with a cool drink, but the hours went by and the last of the patients were dressed before Clover could consider anything so pleasant. She took the diabetic up to the diet kitchen at twelve-thirty exactly and almost wished that Dr Blamine was there to see her efficiency. The others didn't seem to need her and they were quickly absorbed into a group that was shepherded into the pretty dining room of one of the wards.

She looked at her watch. Back at two for the last part of the session. She wasn't sure where the pub would be. When Robin had taken her, she wasn't sure if that was the pub that had been mentioned to her as the best one, and she still had a slightly uneasy feeling about going into strange places on her own.

Anyone can see that I am in uniform, she thought. I can act a part and hide behind my disguise! Salvation Army girls go into the roughest of pubs wearing their distinctive clothes, so why couldn't she visit one within walking distance of the hospital and which would have mostly hospital staff among its customers? She paused by the hospital gates, wondering if she turned left or right. Perhaps it wasn't a good idea after all. Don't be silly, she told herself. If you can't do this, what hope have you of going anywhere interesting without a male escort?

She turned to her right and set off. Hurried footsteps behind her made the hair on her neck prickle automatically. It was silly to be alarmed, she told herself. The footsteps were faster, in long firm strides and with a purpose in them. Clover lengthened her steps without thinking. Before her was an empty road. She must have taken a turning down a side road by mistake, and now she didn't know where to go to find the main road and people.

The cars parked drunkenly on the kerbside, with the near wheels on the pavement were all empty and silent, the windows of the dingy offices were blind. If I look back, I shall show that I think I'm being followed. And if I don't, I shall be scared until he either catches up with me or I can reach that corner, and run—the thoughts raced through her head.

A voice called, but her breath was sharp in her throat and she couldn't hear the words. The steps were faster than hers and nearly behind her. A hand clamped down on her shoulder and she stopped, then turned, striking out with her free hand.

'Clover, you're crazy! It's me!' She saw who it was holding her so tightly and preventing her from hitting out at him again.

'You? Oh!' Dr Blamine towered above her, bemused by her anxiety.

'Yes, me. Now calm down, for heaven's sake.' He still held her close and his arms no longer threatened. 'For God's sake, you're trembling! What are you so frightened about?'

'If you'd been attacked as often as I have during the past day or so, you'd be trembling,' she said, with as much spirit as she could muster. 'I'm sorry I hit you,' she said, hiding her eyes from the now amused smile.

'It was nothing, a mere flea bite,' he said, indulgently. 'If you really want to protect yourself, you need training in the martial arts, my little one.'

'Who wants muscles like that?' she muttered.

He kissed her troubled forehead. 'Don't frown. You will have wrinkles one day if you frown so.'

'It's enough to give me grey hair and wrinkles,' she said, pulling away from him. This would make a very amusing tale for him to tell the beautiful Chantal. She could imagine the silky lashes half hiding the lovely but calculating eyes, glinting with amused malice as he told her the finer points of one young nurse's panic. Chantal might even say that the girl wasn't attractive enough to be followed by a red-blooded man like Darcy, and wasn't she flattering herself to believe it possible?

'Come on, you must be hungry.'

'I'm not,' she lied. 'I thought you were miles away.'

'As you see, I am here, and I *am* hungry. And you are in no fit state to wander in the back streets of London.' He looked up at a street name. 'Is there some place of great historical interest here? Why did you come down this way when I think the place I had in mind was the other way?'

'I like exploring London,' she said, but the corners of her mouth were recovering the quirk of humour that she found hard to hide. The street was revolting, with litter in the kerbside, dreary curtains that badly needed washing at most of the windows and a couple of skinny cats exploring the dustbins long overdue for collection.

'A dustbin circa—what age would you put on it?' His toe raised a dull note as he kicked it gently. 'And this one? Ah, this has a higher note. I think it has less in it, rather like the notes obtained when playing on glasses with water at different levels.' She was laughing now. 'I was good at such things in my young days,' he said. 'But now I am a man with other matters on his mind. The world is a very serious place now, I believe.'

'Not particularly.'

'But you seem to think so. When I see you, there is such a worried look in those lovely green eyes, or there is anger.' The street they reached was civilised, with a newsagents and the glimpse of a real red bus, and on the corner was a barrow overflowing with fruit and vegetables of every kind and size. Flowers spilled from buckets of water and in one were sprays of roses like the ones he had brought to her as a peace offering. He followed her glance. 'You even hated my flowers,' he said.

'No, I didn't. It was just that . . .'

'Just what?' He caught her by the arm. 'Don't go so fast. We nearly missed the door I want. Not of great historical interest, but who wants history when one is hungry?'

The pub was packed and he craned his head to see if there might be two square feet of space. A low wall lay between the pub and the shop next door. Darcy picked her up and sat her on the wall.

'Don't go away. I'll bring some food,' he said, leaving her like a rag doll with her legs dangling over the wall, two feet from the ground.

Clover sat there trying to look as if she sat on pub walls in the less smart areas of London every day of the week. The barrow boy had been relieved by his brother and was looking at the crowd bursting out of the door. He looked up and grinned. 'Room for one more, ducks?'

'Just one. I'm keeping this place.' She put her cloak on the place by the wall and there was room for the man to put his newspaper to reserve his seat.

'Keep it for me, there's a love,' he said and lowered his head to battle his way to the bar.

She was laughing weakly when Darcy Blamine fought a way from the bar with a tray and emerged smiling triumphantly. Clover felt her heart contract painfully. It was stupid to read into their encounter anything that might be of future importance, but this moment was one to cherish, for poignancy, for laughter and for the extraordinary situation in which she found herself. She reached down for the tray and held it on her lap as he sat beside her. 'We can shift along and put the tray between us,' he said.

'No, we can't.' She laughed and nearly spilled the real ale that he had brought to drink with the sandwiches, and the sound was a release of rippling joy. He stared at her for a moment, and she wondered if he was angry. The muscles round his mouth tightened as if he was under stress. 'I have a boyfriend coming to sit there,' she said, her laughter weak and her eyes moist.

'Who? I had no idea you had arranged to meet someone.' The ice was forming again but she saw only the darkness of his eyes.

'Here he comes,' she said, and felt the man beside her relax. 'Take the tray again,' he ordered, and bent down to help the man up on to the wall.

'Thanks, guv.' They sat and ate hot beef sandwiches with lashings of mustard pickle. Clover found that she was very hungry and from the contented silence of her companions she knew that they shared that feeling.

'Good grub, here,' said the barrow boy with his mouth full. 'That's not Bart's uniform,' he said to Clover as soon as he paused for breath. 'I know the old place too well to know that isn't theirs.'

She told him where she was training but didn't say that she was very new, and she felt the flicker of rapport between them as Darcy solemnly answered questions about the internal problems of the man's aunt.

This is stupid. It must be a dream, thought Clover in mild hysteria. I am sitting on a wall with one of the world authorities on endocrinology and a man who sells fruit from a barrow in London! I am eating the most wonderful food I've ever tasted and drinking nectar under the disguise of rather strong beer, and I've never been happier in my life! I know it can't last and that I shall say something or do something that will make him hate me again, but this moment is perfect. I wonder when I shall do a Mary Poppins and take off into the air and find myself back in my bed at Beattie's, with no hope of being with this man who is such a mixture? He can be as arrogant as the devil and as wicked, but he can sit here in deep conversation with this man . . .

She dragged her mind back to what they were saying and it was no shock to discover that Darcy Blamine, apart from all his other talents, was an ice hockey player.

'Do you skate?' he asked. She shook her head.

'You will,' he said. 'It's great.' He turned away again and she thought he had made the polite comment and could now forget her.

'I have to get back soon,' she said. 'I have patients this afternoon.'

'Hang on,' the man said, thrusting his empty tray on to her lap. He rushed back to the barrow and returned with three enormous ripe peaches. 'Here, get that down you, Nurse,' he laughed, handing her one.

They sat with peach juice dripping down their chins, and Clover found a spare tissue for her temporary host. She sucked the peach stone and wiped her fingers with tissue, saying she would wash when she went back to the hospital. Darcy slid from the wall and took the trays, which the barrow boy carried back into the pub. Clover looked down at the ground. It wasn't far away but if she slid down and didn't clear the wall it would mean the end of another pair of tights. Her heart beat faster as she saw the alternative that she couldn't refuse. Darcy's hands encircled her waist and he lifted her clear off the wall. As her feet touched the ground, he bent his head.

'You missed a bit,' he said, with a wicked grin. His mouth touched her cheek and then the corner of her mouth. 'Kisses sweeter than peach juice,' he said, and released her. She blushed but could take no offence at the restrained touch. They waved goodbye to their lunch companion and to Clover's surprise, the hospital was just round the corner.

'I missed my way badly,' she said.

'We all do that at sometime,' he said, looking away. 'What is important is to know where we want to go.'

She glanced at him sharply but could read nothing in his face. 'I must scoop up my charges,' she said. 'Thank you, I did enjoy my lunch break.'

'I must go, too. I have to meet Chantal.'

'Couldn't you have taken her to lunch?' she said. Just because he had seen a Beattie's nurse on her own, he needn't have taken her out for the whole of the lunch break.

'Can you imagine Chantal sitting on a pub wall with a barrow boy?' He turned away and she didn't know if he was ashamed to take the beautiful woman anywhere in that district or if he was laughing . . .

It was becoming very hot again and the patients were restless on the examination beds. Clover went round and took away most of the bed covers, leaving just a sheet to cover each one. An engineer fixed up a fan which helped to circulate the air, and iced drinks were brought in on a trolley supplied by the hospital friends. Clover had an aunt who helped in this way in the local hospital in the north and now she saw the value of their work, supplying simple comforts that were not provided by the health service, but which made all the difference to the humanity and service of a large institution.

As the afternoon came to its end, she wondered where Darcy Blamine and Chantal would go that evening. She also spared a thought for Sister Scott. Had she and Dr Crown come to a better understanding? From the glances exchanged that morning, it might be so. Clover smiled at the thought of the illusive Dr Richard Crown being snared for good and having to end his days of flirtation and dalliance.

I suppose that most of the sisters at Beattie's are young and attractive because they tend to marry early and make room for the next generation of eager Florence Nightingales, Clover reasoned. I might be like Sister Scott one day, she thought. If I'm any good, I might be a sister at Beattie's.

But the idea didn't thrill her half as much as it would have done a couple of months earlier. It was what she had wanted for so long. Was this a feeling of anti-climax now that she was doing what her heart and head had told her was right for her, for years? Or had Darcy Blamine destroyed her ambition and taken away her hopes for the future?

Perhaps when he has gone, perhaps when I know that he is married to Chantal or living with her, I can settle for what is left and still be happy, she mused. It still didn't make her feel any more hopeful.

'Nurse, I think that all of your patients have gone but one. I've sent for a taxi for him as it isn't worth bringing the minibus back all this way,' the Bart's sister announced.

'Do I have to go with him?'

'No, but if you want a lift back to Beattie's, the cab will be here in half an hour. If you'd help clear the blankets away, you can catch it.' Sister glanced round the room. It was incredible how much mess some of the consultants made, however minor the examination. She went away mumbling about the importance of training students to put things away, and Clover was inclined to agree. She had seen doctors leave the clinical room in an awful mess and then blame the nearest nurse if everything wasn't to their liking. Just like Darcy Blamine, she thought, severely, reminding herself to think only of his bad points and not of the sweetness of that lopsided smile and the wonderful strength of the man.

She folded blankets and wiped up spilled water from one of the jugs of iced water, tidied the array of surgical instruments that were a part of the test and took the sheets to the nurse on duty in the outpatients department next door, where they joined the others from that department on a linen trolley. It took ages and when she had done, she felt hot and sticky.

'Any chance of a shower?' she asked a porter. He directed her to an empty room used by surgeons after a clinic, but unused today. Thankfully, she slipped out of uniform and showered in cool water, used the towels stored there and dressed in the casual clothes she had brought with her. Her watch showed that she had plenty of time, but she seemed to have taken ages over the clearing. Clover looked again and held the watch to her ear. It had stopped.

She had changed because she was hot—she had no intention of staying in town for the evening. Her experience at lunch time had shown her that she was not ready to venture out in the big city without an escort. She finished dressing, knowing that she was too late to have a lift in the taxi. 'How do I get back to Beattie's?' she asked a nurse when she emerged from the shower room.

'Beattie's? Is that north London?' came the reply.

The porter at the entrance thought she was a visitor until she explained that she had brought patients that morning. He looked at a note among the many on the desk. 'Ah, Nurse Dylan. Thought I remembered the name. Car for you about now I shouldn't wonder. Sit over there and you'll see it come.'

So the taxi hadn't yet arrived. Clover didn't know if she felt relief or not. It was too nice an evening to go back and look at notes, watch the television or mend her jeans. The summer dress she had brought with her was soft and flowing, with pastel colours merging down the skirt as if a rainbow had been washed and the colours had run. The top was scoop-necked and sleeveless and her sandals were glossy blue-green. Her hair was still damp from the badly aligned shower and she wore no make-up but a soft lipstick and a touch of eye shadow. All dressed up and nowhere to go, she thought, sadly. When the car comes, I'll go back and ring Robin. She couldn't recall his number and knew that it wasn't among the hospital numbers in the telephone directory.

On an impulse, she went to the porter and asked him to tell the car to wait when it came, as she had to make a telephone call. She dialled the number of the nurses' hostel at Beattie's and hoped that one of her set would answer it. Some of them might be in their rooms during the late tea break and they would know if Rosalyn was off duty. She was the only other person at Beattie's who knew Robin's telephone number. The phone went on ringing, and Clover had nearly given up hope of anyone answering it when she heard Rosalyn's voice.

'Ros, this is Clover. I'm still at the hospital but

I'm off duty now. Have you got Robin's telephone number?'

'Oh, hello.' Rosalyn seemed less than thrilled to hear her voice. 'As a matter of fact, Robin rang me just now.'

'Great. When's he coming over?'

'Well, actually, I'm on my way to change and then I'm meeting him.'

'Fine. How long will you be?' Clover hesitated, suddenly realising that she wasn't included in the invitation. 'Sorry, I didn't think. He asked you for a date?'

'Yes.' Rosalyn sounded relieved and spoke rather fast. 'Well, I didn't know when you'd be back or if you had other plans for the evening—I was off, and he was at a loose end, so I said, OK, let's go out.'

'I'm glad,' said Clover, half believing her own conventional reply. 'I shall window-shop and come back later. Love to Robin.'

She hung up and turned to the entrance hall again, her eyes recording nothing of her surroundings. Even dear old Robin had plans that didn't include her, and Richard Crown wasn't the kind of man she could telephone or he would take too much for granted. In any case, he seemed to have gone back to Sister Bridget Scott and Clover had no wish to have his company except on a very casual basis.

She thought of Chantal. Her day of professional work would be over now, unless she was dining with a highpowered executive, or a man like Darcy

Blamine. I can never compete with someone like that, she thought. Chantal could look elegant in a sack and probably make it fashionable!

The soft folds of her own dress did nothing to raise her spirits and she wished that the car would come quickly. She gave a start. It wasn't just for her. There should be a patient somewhere, waiting to be taken back to Beattie's. How could she forget her duty in her day-dreaming?

'Do you know where the patient is who I am taking back to Beattie's?' she asked the porter.

'They've all gone, Nurse.'

'But you said there would be a car for me. I doubt if the hospital would bother to collect me when I had already been told to make my own way back if the patients had left.'

'I don't know about that, Nurse. I gave you the message I had.'

She went back to the hard bench, wondering what to do. If the patient *had* gone, she could wait all night and no car would come for her. And the sunshine outside was beckoning her to walk in its soft rays and soothe her worries away.

If I go and the car comes, Admin will be furious if they have to pay for a wasted journey. But I shall waste all my time if I stay here on this bench! Make up your mind, she told herself. It all added up to her basic inadequacy. She smiled slightly and murmured the silly rhyme on the jug. 'I'm just a glow worm and I'll never be a star,' she said aloud.

'Oh, so that charming little jug was yours, was it?' Darcy Blamine stood before her, in a trimly cut linen shirt of dark blue and close-fitting trousers. His hair was wet from a shower and curled over his brow in a very undisciplined way. Clover blushed and looked away, muttering a whispered greeting. The one man she wanted to avoid when she was doing something stupid, like talking to herself, *would* be the one to appear and even recognise what she was saying. It also ruled out the possibility of her removing the little jug from his room or from the kitchen without him knowing that it was hers.

'I didn't expect to see you again today,' she said coldly.

'I appear all over the place,' he said, smiling.

'I thought you had business at the Research Centre.'

'So I had, but certain things wouldn't stay out of my mind and I was restless.' He looked down at her bent head. 'Don't you ever get restless, Nurse Dylan?' She looked up, aware of the mocking tone as he said Nurse Dylan.

'I haven't been in this job for more than a month or so. How can I be restless?' Now she felt wary of him—what was he up to?

'You seemed so when you were deciding whether to make that phone call,' he said, calmly. 'Tell me, what arrangement did you come to that made you look so sad?'

'I'm not sad. I'm just wondering if I should wait any longer for the car that the porter said was to fetch me. I have an uneasy feeling that there has been a mix-up. Perhaps I should ring Beattie's and ask them if the car is coming or if the porter was referring to the one that left earlier.' She was acutely aware of his eyes. They seemed even more deeply blue today against the dark shirt. She got up and walked to the telephone booth again.

'Don't bother to do that. I assure you that there is a car at your disposal.' His glance took in the details of her bare legs with their golden tan and the soft folds of her skirt, outlining the curve of her thighs as the fabric clung to her in the breeze from the open door.

'Oh, I see,' she smiled. 'You are waiting for the same car. Are you going back to Beattie's?'

'I'm not sure. What do you suggest?'

'Me? If the car comes to take me back, I suppose I'd better use it. If it doesn't, I can take the bus into the West End,' she said, sounding more confident than she felt.

He raised his eyebrows. 'Are you meeting Richard?'

'No. I thought that as I am off duty and in the heart of London, I might as well make use of the time to see a little more of the city.

'No date? Not even with that rather importunate youth who came out of your room on one memorable occasion?' Darcy sounded sceptical.

'I told you that he is a friend of my brother, or he was some time ago. He comes to the house when my parents are in England, and I can't avoid meeting him,' Clover snapped.

'You seemed rather involved when I saw you,' Darcy said, mildly, but his face hardened as if the memory angered him.

Oh, don't let him bring that up again, she thought desperately. After their carefree lunch, she had hoped that even if he thought her an unlikely success as a nurse, he might forget the other times when he had appeared unexpectedly and at quite the wrong moment.

'As you say, you appear all over the place,' she said, bitterly, 'And you don't give me any credit for the truth.'

'It's difficult to forget some things, Clover.'

She looked up, expecting to see the brows in a censorious line, but his face showed no sign of anger. 'It's difficult to forget how you looked when I saw you in the kitchen. It's difficult to forget how you were, running away from that young man—and it's difficult to forget you sitting on a wall, with mustard pickle on your chin.'

She almost ran to the door, her cheeks hot with sudden colour. How could he be so heartless when she wanted him so badly? How could he refer to every occasion when she had been at a disadvantage? The memory of that time in the telephone room was bad enough! She'd been so scantily dressed that perhaps he could be forgiven for thinking that she wandered about like that to attract the attention of men.

But she must have looked very much worse when she ran from Alex, trying to gather her dress together to preserve her modesty . . .

Where was the damned car? She stared out into the dusty courtyard where spirals of air took leaves and scraps of paper into a small whirlwind. Darcy was behind her and she had to escape. But where could she go with the certainty of not seeing him again. 'I'm leaving nursing,' she heard herself say. 'I'm not going to be any good and everyone finds me funny.'

'Everyone?'

'Well, you do, and if you do, then others will take their cue from you. I think I'll join the army,' she said.

He laughed, and the sound made her want to turn to him and join in his laughter. There was no mockery there, but rather as if he appreciated some gem of wit, but she convinced herself that he was still laughing at her and not with her.

'If you take the car, it won't be wasted,' she said, with dignity. 'Excuse me, please, Dr Blamine. I have better things to do with my time than to stay here to amuse you.'

'The car is over there,' he said. She looked at the line of cars parked by the wall of the hospital. No car had arrived since they stood by the door and the cars were in the slots kept for members of staff. 'The grey one,' he said, and she recognised the car in which she had been taken from the Falcon in the rain the night that she was to have spent the evening with Richard Crown.

'But that's *your* car.'

'Of course. You didn't think I'd wait around for cabs, did you?'

'I suppose not.' He wasn't the type to wait around for anything. One look at that arrogant jaw should convince anyone of that fact. But his face had no arrogance as he unlocked the door and stood back, waiting for her to make up her mind whether to get in or not. 'Have you made up your mind where you want to go?'

'Back to Beattie's, I suppose,' she sighed, resigned.

'I thought you wanted to be away from Beattie's as soon as possible? Surely every moment away is good if you hate it so much?' Now he was laughing at her again!

She climbed in and he put out a hand to make sure that her skirt wasn't caught in the door, letting his fingers trace the line of her calf as he did so. A thrill of awareness flooded through her and when he was beside her in the car, she held her breath. Don't let him know how I feel about him, she prayed. I can't bear much more and if he knows I love him, he will only laugh at me and chalk up one more conquest. I must fix my mind on Chantal and remember that she is the one he loves. He didn't start the engine, and she glanced up in surprise.

'You still haven't said where you want to go,' he said, patiently. 'You suppose you ought to go back to Beattie's, but that isn't worth considering on such an evening. I have no intention of going back yet, so I'm afraid you'll just have to tag along with me for a while, if you can bear to do so.'

'Where are you going?'

'Richard suggested St Katharine's Dock.' She widened her eyes. 'He seems to think it quite a place and as I have so little time in England, I must make the most of every opportunity to see every-thing that this city can offer.'

'Of course,' she said. 'I was forgetting that you and Dr Delonde will be going back soon.'

'Will you take pity on a lonely man, Clover?' A shiver of suppressed sensuality ran down her spine. If he could possibly be lonely, she would gladly give up everything to make his life happy, to fill it with laughter and love and caring. She nodded, but smiled as if to doubt that he could be lonely. 'You don't believe me?' he asked.

'No. You have everything,' she said with certain-ty. The car nosed through the stream of rush-hour traffic and left the bustle of the city. Soon the cobbled waterside road made Darcy slacken speed.

'It should be somewhere near,' Clover said. 'I can see Tower Bridge from here.'

'We'll park here and walk, if those silly little sandals can take you over the cobbles.'

'I could walk for miles in them,' she boasted and promptly stumbled.

'You need a doctor,' he said, tucking her arm in his and taking her to a smoother patch of the walkway. They walked along by the river and found the still sombre place, where unhappy victims of a more savage age were taken through Traitor's Gate.

Darcy seemed to know a lot about the history of the Tower and Clover was happy to let him talk, to watch his face change expression and to share the precious moments with him, while her sad heart beat the requiem of her love. He's going away, he's going away with Chantal and I shall never see him again—the words thudded in her ears, deafening her.

'You're not listening,' he said at last.

'I am,' she protested rather unconvincingly.

'But, like me, you are hungry. I'm glad to see how fully you've recovered from your jabs. Let's eat now and walk again later.' He led her to the dock that had been restored so well that it looked as it must have done when the square-rigged sailing vessels plied their trade. They must have sailed majestically down the Thames to the sea and to lands far away, taken by wind and tide and bearing rich cargoes back to St Katharine's. The tall masts of many ships stood against the sky and although the many small shops around the water front were modern inside, selling everything from sticking plaster to Guardsmen souvenir dolls, the ambience of the area was good. Clover sighed with pleasure as she saw the old ships, restored to their orginal glory. She stopped by a weatherbeaten Thames barge with its dark red sails and sombre paintwork.

'One day, I'm going to see the Thames barge race,' she said. 'I love old boats.'

'The Tall Ships race might be good to follow, too,' he said, thoughtfully.

'Oh, *yes!*' She said it before she could stop herself. What would he think? It sounded as if she was forcing an invitation from him.

'We eat here.' He spoke quietly, directing her to an old warehouse that had been converted to a restaurant. Nothing was said until the upper floor had been reached and the pretty waitress, dressed in Dickensian clothes to carry on the theme of the restaurant, nodded as Darcy gave her his name and led them to a table by a window overlooking the boats.

'You booked a table!' Clover sat down and stared at him. Was he so sure that she would come with him? Could no woman refuse him? Then she thought she knew the answer. Chantal had been too busy or preoccupied to keep a date with him and he had snatched at her company because he didn't know who else to ask.

'I like to know I can find a seat. We can't spend our lives sitting on brick walls, eating sandwiches, can we?' He smiled as if pleased when she ordered seafood cocktail. 'We have superlative seafood in Canada,' he said. 'We also have lots of sailing and water sports.' She smiled, politely and began to eat. The white wine was cool and the glass clouded as he poured it from the iced bottle.

'You really should learn to skate,' he commented. 'It's wonderful when the river freezes and the stars shine. We have parties by the river and build huge fires beside the ice, with roast potatoes, steaks and fish.'

'Does Chantal go in for such activities?' Clover asked coolly.

'Can you imagine her getting her hands cold if she could avoid it?' It wasn't said tenderly—as if she was special, in her fragility and loveliness, and could never be exposed to the rigours of winter as other mortals could be—but rather as if Darcy Blamine had no time for people like that.

If he loves her, he must accept that she can't do everything he wants, Clover thought wryly. Chantal has a very definite mind of her own and they will have to give and take a little if they marry. Somehow Clover couldn't imagine that such forced harmony would prevail for a lifetime.

'What do your friends think of training?'

'What do you mean?' She knew he didn't want to discuss his private feelings for Chantal, but this was a sudden switch. The steak arrived and when they had been served with courgettes and broccoli spears, he repeated the question as if it was important.

'We all enjoy the work,' she said non-committally.

'You said you might leave.' Darcy pressed for her answer.

'I know.' She bent over her food. 'I didn't make a very happy start.'

'And the others? Did they suffer in some way, too? Or was it that you felt weak because you were ill?'

Clover carefully cut a piece of steak into a cube and then in two again. She divided a head of broccoli spear as carefully as if her life depended on the two pieces being equal. How could she answer when her heart cried out for his love, his attention and his lifelong companionship?

'Everything seemed to go wrong,' she murmured. 'Vilma was a little sad, too,' she said, determined not to show her true feelings.

'And now?' He seemed genuinely concerned.

'She has decided to marry her fiancé before he goes away. They will be apart for months, but she seems to think they will be happier knowing that they are married and can be together as much as possible.' Clover's voice was becoming husky. Talking about another girl in love did nothing to help her.

'Would you do that, if you had to be apart from the man you married?' The lights were coming on like glow-worms among the boats out in the dusk and as the restaurant filled, the table by the window with the muted red candle-lamp seemed remote from the world.

'Of course I would. Any girl worth anything would wait if she had to do so.' It was said with such certainty that Clover surprised herself.

'And if he couldn't wait and wanted you for all time, what then?'

The glow of the candle made bronze lights shine in her hair and Darcy seemed to come closer across the table. He took her hand and smoothed the silky skin at the back of her wrist, making her shudder with the implication that he wanted her.

I must resist, she told herself. He wants me at this moment, but what of tomorrow? Could I face the world, face life, if he took me and then callously threw me away?

'It's the time for truth,' he said, gently.

'For me or for you?' Clover murmured.

'For us,' he said, simply. 'Can't you see that I love you? Can't you see that from the moment I saw you, I wanted you? What man would not want you as you were when I first saw you?' She lowered her gaze, ashamed that he remembered. 'And what man could resist you, seeing you at work, with that tiny frown of concentration that I wanted to kiss away?'

'I thought you despised me,' she whispered.

'First I desired you and was angry because I believed that you were going to another.' He stood up and came to her side and they faced the window and the twinkling lights. His shoulder was warm and strong, his mouth on her hair, gentle.

'I began to love you and couldn't ask you to give up your career for me. I have to go back to Canada. I shall be away for a long time, but there are such things as airlines. Could you do as Vilma is doing? I can't ask you to wait for me until you finish your training. That would be more than I could bear.'

Clover blushed in the dim light, knowing that his passion would be all-consuming and that she must make a decision that would turn her world upside-down.

'You must have leave soon and we can be married before I go back.' He put a hand under her chin and kissed her, oblivious of the people in the room. 'Unless, you could give up your training and come with me. In Canada, you could start again and we could be together. It wouldn't be the same as Beattie's though, and you might miss your friends.' His body was rigid with waiting for her answer and she knew that he was desperately afraid that she wouldn't want to leave England.

Clover felt that she had gained a strength that she

had never thought possible, and now she knew her own power. She smiled, tenderly, her love and complete commitment shining in her eyes.

'If I can train and be ready to help you, I will follow you wherever you are. If you want me to give it all up, I will do that, if you really love me.'

He buried his face in her hair, unable to speak and she knew that nothing mattered but their love.

Doctor Nurse Romances

Amongst the intense emotional pressures of modern medical life, doctors and nurses often find romance. Read about their lives and loves in the other three Doctor Nurse titles available this month.

ITALIAN NURSE
by Lydia Balmain

'I expect my nurses to be women of intelligence, not blonde ragamuffins,' Doctor Rodrigo Vitale tells Staff Nurse Sharon Craig on her arrival at his hospital above the Bay of Naples. After such an unfortunate introduction how can she hope to convince him that she's a competent nurse and not a dizzy blonde?

INTENSIVE AFFAIR
by Ann Jennings

I always get what I want…That's Dr Richard West's proud boast, and looking at all the expensive equipment he's acquired for the Intensive Care Unit at County General, Sister Charmian Williams can well believe it. Surely such a brilliant, good-looking and persuasive man can be refused nothing? So when he turns his attentions to Charmian what hope does she have of resistance…

NURSE IN DOUBT
by Denise Robertson

Life in orthopaedics Outpatients is never dull for Nurse Imogen Brent, particularly when she has to contend with the demanding Dr Roger Wemyss every day. But when she is betrayed by her boyfriend, Roger Wemyss is the only person to show her any sympathy and Imogen is surprised to find that there is another side to her difficult boss…

Mills & Boon
the rose of romance

4 Doctor Nurse Romances
FREE

Coping with the daily tragedies and ordeals of a busy hospital, and sharing the satisfaction of a difficult job well done, people find themselves unexpectedly drawn together. Mills & Boon Doctor Nurse Romances capture perfectly the excitement, the intrigue and the emotions of modern medicine, that so often lead to overwhelming and blissful love. By becoming a regular reader of Mills & Boon Doctor Nurse Romances you can enjoy EIGHT superb new titles every two months plus a whole range of special benefits: your very own personal membership card, a free newsletter packed with recipes, competitions, bargain book offers, plus big cash savings.

**AND an Introductory FREE GIFT for YOU.
Turn over the page for details.**

**Fill in and send this coupon back today
and we'll send you
4 Introductory
Doctor Nurse Romances yours to keep**

FREE

At the same time we will reserve a
subscription to Mills & Boon
Doctor Nurse Romances for you. Every
two months you will receive the latest
8 new titles, delivered direct to your door.
You don't pay extra for delivery. Postage and
packing is always completely Free.
There is no obligation or commitment –
you receive books only for
as long as you want to.

**It's easy! Fill in the coupon below and return it to
MILLS & BOON READER SERVICE, FREEPOST, P.O. BOX 236,
CROYDON, SURREY CR9 9EL.**

**Please note: READERS IN SOUTH AFRICA write to
Mills & Boon Ltd., Postbag X3010,
Randburg 2125, S. Africa.**

- - - - - - - - - - - - - - - - - -

FREE BOOKS CERTIFICATE

**To: Mills & Boon Reader Service, FREEPOST, P.O. Box 236,
Croydon, Surrey CR9 9EL.**

Please send me, free and without obligation, four Dr. Nurse Romances, and reserve a
Reader Service Subscription for me. If I decide to subscribe I shall receive, following my free
parcel of books, eight new Dr. Nurse Romances every two months for £8.00, post and
packing free. If I decide not to subscribe, I shall write to you within 10 days. The free books
are mine to keep in any case. I understand that I may cancel my subscription at any time
simply by writing to you. I am over 18 years of age.
Please write in BLOCK CAPITALS.

Name _____

Address _____

_____

_____ Postcode _____

SEND NO MONEY — TAKE NO RISKS

*Remember, postcodes speed delivery. Offer applies in UK only and is not valid to
present subscribers. Mills & Boon reserve the right to exercise discretion
in granting membership. If price changes are necessary you will be noti-
fied. Offer expires 31st December 1984.*

8DN

EP